Created To Rule

Pastor Grace Oby Johnson

DEDICATIONS

To the *Eternal Godhead* who is everything to me and has given me access to some of His choicest Servants who have enriched my life in the ministry.

To the *Holy Spirit of God,* whose tutelage has been my greatest resource; whose wisdom and revelations (Rhema) guided me through the years of incubating and writing this book.

To the *youth of our world*—may your generation never have to reject the Principles of God's word which is able to not only create wealth but to perpetuate wealth in your generations for the furtherance of God's Kingdom on earth.

To the *Body of Christ* globally who are laboring under the burden of limited resources due to her inability to discern the sources of their beliefs on *Wealth Creation* – may this book enlighten the eyes of your understanding and set you free from the lies of the devil. May this book rekindle love in you for God's word – the Bible.

WEALTH CREATION SERIES

CREATED TO RULE

CONTENTS

Section Two

Section Three

ACKNOWLEDGMENTS

This book has taken more than 25 years of my life to incubate and three years to write, and many people encouraged me during the entire process.

No individual succeeds alone ...many gifted people contributed to the completion of this book and I wish I could acknowledge everyone who was part of the process. Though this is not possible due to space, I must mention that every person's effort is deeply appreciated.

Some were such glowing examples just by their dedication to the Lord Jesus Christ and their ministries.

To Dr. Mike Murdock whose products got me out of seven years of depression, and rekindled my love for the work of the ministry, thanks for believing in me.

To Pastor E.A Adeboye whose counsel and prayers brought me into a wealthy place.

To Pastor Matthew Ashimolowo who God used to lift up my spirit when I thought all was over. I appreciate the long hours of phone calls from London at your own expense, just because you discerned a Jewel in me that must not be buried. You are a true Friend.

To Dr. Reuben Ezemadu, you are a Friend that sticks closer than a brother.

To my children, Uchechukwu and Chinwenwa who are God's blessings on my life.

To all the members of our ministry at *Logos Aflame Ministries* in Lagos, Nigeria and around the world. It is impossible to mention everyone's name – thank you for being the Holy Spirit's theatre for my practicals. May God's kingdom experience a perpetuation of wealth in your generation through your obedience to His word.

FOREWORD

When The Wise Talk, The Wise Listen.
Every Problem in your life is simply a wisdom problem. God creates seasons but your discoveries schedule them. The dominant purpose of wisdom is to create order in your personal life and world.

That's why this collection of wisdom could forever change your life. CREATED TO RULE... is a Master Handbook on uncommon success ......and could unlock wealth in every part of your life. Few authors and teachers possess this vast understanding of scriptural founded wealth. Pastor Grace lives what she teaches. She walks with a remarkable anointing for uncommon favor. The secrets within these pages could be the Golden Key you have searched a lifetime to find. Especially when you grasp the profound mystery known to the wealthy about investing. Her many years of scriptural research combined with her own personal testimony will birth unparallel hope in you as you observe her addiction to the Voice of God and willingness to obey it.

Pastor Grace is my personal friend ...... and very respected leader in the Body of Christ. Uncommon Achievers are familiar with her marvelous Faith Life and her spiritual discernment. She is more than a Supernatural Success Story. She is pouring out her life around the world.....unlocking The Destiny of those who passionately pursue her mentorship.

Her students will celebrate the Access she has provided. More than anything, they will become Trophies on Display of what an Uncommon Mentor can unlock in your life. Mentorship is Wisdom without the wait. Mentorship is Success without the Pain. In writing this book, Pastor Grace has provided the global family of God a Miracle Door to another season. For this, we shall always be grateful.

Dr. Mike Murdock.
Wisdom Center
Dallas TX.
U.S.A.

PREFACE

A Great Abomination: Beggars On Horses And Kings on Foot. What a reversal of roles and a perversion of order. The Lord has made us His children, Princes and Kings. Yet in everyday life we see servants on horses and Princes on foot; Eccl. 10:7.

In this book, "Created To Rule" Pastor Grace Oby Johnson has carefully laid out the principles and precepts for children of God to get on horses and rule. To Have Dominion.

What we lost in the Garden of Eden was restored at the Cross of Calvary.

Children of God are deceived and held captive by deception of the devil. This book should open your eyes to see where you really belong as a child of the Kingdom.

Sadly, slaves have hijacked the principles and reinforced a great lie to their own advantage. I pray that as you read this book the scales will drop and you will reign as God intended and designed – as a Servant-King and Joint Heir.

Using your wealth and power to serve humanity by advancing the cause of the gospel.

God bless you.

Pastor E. A. Adeboye
General Overseer,
Redeemed Christian Church of God.
Lagos - Nigeria

INTRODUCTION

Created to Rule came to me as a result of several years of observing Christians struggle with *ignorance* in the area of their authority over God's creation. Christians have been taught that faith is passive; that they need not develop their mental capabilities, especially in the "Third World" countries. So much attention is dedicated to developing one's spirit that the development of the mind is neglected. This has led to poverty in the Church over the centuries. There is such a vehement resistance in the Church regarding the issue of prosperity and wealth. I suppose people are not as opposed to teaching the principles of prosperity as they are to enforcing those principles. People would rather believe that God could drop bread from heaven than act on God's principles for prosperity. Their financial life is totally extricated from their spiritual life. They are blind to the fact that money is needed for the preaching of the gospel and that money answers all things, as King Solomon says in the Bible.

It would appear that the poorest people on earth are Christians, especially the Bible-believing ones. There is great ignorance in the Church body and this lack of mental development has even led to some life-threatening health conditions. Many Church people are sick, but they prefer to stand in healing lines rather than be informed about habits that lead to poor health conditions.

Being ignorant of God's purpose for instituting marriage has led to many broken relationships. People rarely seek God's wisdom in their marriages. In many societies, Christian marriages are based on the cultures of the people rather than on God's Word.

The Bible is such a gold mine for any Christian pursuing wisdom. It says, *"wisdom is the principal thing"* (Proverbs 4:7). The wisdom of God in the Bible is sufficient enough to put anyone, regardless of his level of creativity, at the top of the ladder of success in this life.

God set in motion *laws* on earth that would sustain His world. For six days in the book of Genesis, God created all things, including man and *rested* on the seventh day. The Bible says that God ceased from all His works and rested. Does that mean that God is no longer in the business of creation? New babies are still being born and creative miracles still take place today. What His *rest* means is that He set in motion laws that have continued to sustain His creation right from the beginning. He does not lift a finger to amend anything because the laws of nature He put in place are sustaining everything. It is man's responsibility to discover these laws and obey them. Ignorance of these laws is the cause of poverty, sickness and depression among Christians. There are laws of prosperity in God's Word, which when obeyed will bring about prosperity. There are also laws guiding marriage, laws to good health, and so on. Obedience to God's instructions is the key to your miracles.

Moreover, God's relationship with man is based on *covenants*. From Genesis to Revelation, man could not relate to God without sacrifices – this is one of the ways of ratifying God's relationship with man. The terms of a covenant are binding laws.

All I am trying to say is that we must discover the wisdom in God's Word that will make us prosper. God created man to rule over the rest of His creation. Man, created in the image of God, is the wisest of all God's creatures. God instructed man to take dominion over the rest of His creation and rule over them. In many cases, man does not 'look' like he is in dominion, even after the new birth experience and this is as a result of *ignorance*.

Created to Rule intends to show God's people that there is provision in God's covenant for them to rule over the present earth. In the beginning, God did not create this earth for the devil and his agents. It is erroneous to believe that after the fall of Adam, God abandoned His whole creation to the devil. This is what this book is out to address. This is the second in the series of my writings on Wealth Creation. The first book is entitled, *"Living In God's Abundance – A Life Style."* *Created to Rule* can only bless you if you diligently follow the instructions in it with an open heart. The primary focus of this book is how the believer in Christ Jesus can rule in dominion over the realm of wealth for Kingdom purposes. There are so many misconceptions about the Christian possessing wealth. In some quarters it is a taboo to think of a "true Christian" becoming rich. It must be emphasized that such religious beliefs have not deterred God's people from becoming rich and blessed. This book debunks such lies from religious demons.

Created to Rule is a teaching on wealth creation based on Bible principles. It is all about creating *extras* for God's kingdom. Wealth is power. With wealth many things are possible. You can preach the gospel on air 24 hours a day, seven days a week, all year round. You can own a private jet for preaching the gospel around the world. Anything is possible! I chose early in my faith-walk to possess wealth for the Kingdom of God, so I set out with a willing and open mind to study the secrets of the wealthy. My greatest discovery was in the *Word* of God, the Bible. Though it took most of my prime years to discover these secrets, I am glad I finally did. It is more rewarding to toe the path of discovery than to sit back enviously watching others enjoy wealth.

Your first step towards wealth creation is to **review all your beliefs** regarding the question about Christian believers possessing wealth, and go on to **delete all religious arguments** that are unscriptural. Some of these beliefs are based on misinterpretations of some portions of the Bible, while others are just traditional beliefs of men - myths passed down over time. None of this makes the scriptures ineffective to the one who discovers God's original intention for possessing wealth. In this book, we shall carefully examine God's thoughts on wealth creation, so I urge you to keep an open mind for the greatest discovery of your life!

This entire book is based on God's instruction in Genesis 1:28 to the first created man – Adam – to *"... have dominion* (rule) *over the fish of the sea, over the birds of the air, and over every living thing that moves on the earth...".* I guarantee you a truly great discovery on wealth creation.

SECTION ONE

Discover the three spheres of rulership ordained by God for man to be successful on earth.

CHAPTER ONE

THREE REALMS OF RULERSHIP:

Ruling Over the Sea

> *"Then God blessed them, and God said to them, "Be fruitful and multiply; fill the earth and subdue it; have dominion (rule) over the fish of the sea, over the birds of the air, and over every living thing that moves on the earth."* Genesis 1:28

Most nations have these three realms of Defense in their military: the Marine force, the Air force and the Ground force. From the above scripture, God specified these realms for rulership for mankind. In the introduction of this book I stated that although God has destined man to rule over the rest of His creation, man does not 'look' like it in many quarters. The Bible makes it plain that from the very beginning of creation, God made provision for man's wellbeing. God first of all provided for every need of mankind before bringing man on stage. Man was created on the very last day of creation. And after creating man, God gave him authority to *rule* over all His creation. According to the above passage of the Bible, God gave man authority to have dominion and rule over the following three realms:

1. The Sea
2. The Air
3. The land

Watching the start of the war in Iraq in April 2003 on the Cable Network News (CNN), I personally learnt a lot of lessons on the strategies employed by the American – led Coalition Forces:

(a) They never struck at their target until they gathered enough intelligence, (This demonstrates the place of information in the time of preparation).
(b) They moved closer to the battleground, advancing to their target – the *land* of the enemy.... Took the battle to their enemy's camp.
(c) The *sea* passage was employed for movement of heavy-duty equipment and the Marine Corps.
(d) The actual battle began with *air* raids.

The Air Force raided every suspected target, jolting their enemies on the ground and also making way for the ground forces to advance and occupy. As the battle progressed, the Marine Corps were sent in to clear the seaway, defending and protecting the ground troops, while preventing any attack through the sea.

At wartime, the sea is the best option for bringing in food and other relief materials to the displaced and the military. Heavy-duty ammunitions are also transported by sea.

The three Realms of rulership were brought into play for the attained success of that war. Likewise, God intends for His children to rule and have dominion over these three realms of life.

The Realm of the Sea.

The realm of the *sea* is the realm of *commerce* – the realm of exchange. In certain instances the Bible speaks of the sea as representing human beings. Prophetically, it speaks of nations.

"Then I stood on the sand of the sea. And I saw a beast rising up out of the sea..." Revelation 13:1

The beast in this instance is a political leader rising from the sea of people.

"Daniel spoke, saying, "I saw in my vision by night, and behold, the four winds of heaven were stirring up the Great Sea. And four great beasts came up from the sea, each different from the other." Daniel 7:2-3

These four great beasts are world leaders and the Great Sea blown by the four winds of heaven is speaking prophetically of the peoples of the whole earth.

The Bible also speaks of the Sea as an avenue of merchandise (commerce).

"For the king had merchant ships at sea with the fleet of Hiram. Once every three years the merchant ships came bringing gold, silver, ivory, apes, and monkeys. So King Solomon surpassed all the kings of the earth in riches and wisdom." 1 Kings 10:22-23

The entire chapter of Ezekiel 27 speaks of merchandising on the Sea of Tarshish. Though this chapter of the Bible focuses on God's judgment on the nation of Tyre, our emphasis is on the sea being an avenue for commerce.

"Elders of Gebal and its wise men were in you to caulk your seams; all the ships of the sea and their oarsmen were in you to market your merchandise." Ezekiel 27: 9

"The ships of Tarshish were carriers of your merchandise. You were filled and very glorious in the midst of the seas. Your oarsmen brought you into

*many waters, but the east wind broke you in the midst
of the seas."* Ezekiel 27: 25-26

In today's global economy, the sea also brings wealth to
nations. The seaports of any nation are powerful realms of commerce. Nations with seaports engage in much trading that brings
them great wealth from other nations.

The Marketplace Christian
The sea here prophetically represents Christians in the marketplace, professionals, and businesspeople of all levels.

What am I trying to say? God intends that His own should rule
over this area of life. The Christian in the marketplace should,
without fear or doubt, pursue dominance in his field of business.
This is God's will for you. As we shall see in later chapters of this
book, God established a division of labor between the Priesthood
and the rest of the Israelites. While the Priesthood focused on their
work in the House of God, the rest of Israel made available material provisions for them through their tithes and offerings (sacrifices). Each tribe was commanded by God to provide land for
living as well as pastureland for the Priesthood within their own
inheritance. Their tithes and offerings were to sustain the
Priesthood. The Priesthood was not allowed to live in seclusion:
they were to live among the communities of Israel on properties
provided by each tribe. By this method, the presence of God was
found among the tribes. This was intended to bring about a kind of
partnership in God's Kingdom work.

The Church today should function within the principles laid
down by God. While the minister of the gospel pays attention to
equipping the saints, the saints in turn should play the role of
providing financially and materially for their ministers. In my years
of ministry, I found that a lot of believers became jealous of their
ministers and many withheld their financial support. Some who felt
wounded by the life style of other ministers also spoke spitefully of
every other minister. All of these are the ploys of the devil to frus-
trate the work of God.

There are very few Christians who understand their partnership with their minister in the Kingdom business. Your calling may be *giving* as recorded in Romans 12:8: *"...he who gives, with liberality..."* This should go beyond your tithes and offerings. I learnt of a Christian businessman who by the leading of the Lord raised a particular investment for the purpose of giving regularly to the gospel. And there are others who have come to this level of understanding in the gospel. Their giving to the Lord is viewed as investments and they give without much struggling.

Mention must be made of the need for the Church in Africa and other Third World countries to teach that not all are called to pastor. Some business people who are sound in the faith can be on the air and preach the gospel. We see such glowing examples in the Church in America; not all the television preachers pastor Churches, but they have businesses that sustain their television programs, even though they raise partners who add to the support.

As a Pastor with over 25 years experience (at the time of writing this book), I have come to learn that money is critical in the preaching of the gospel, be it in the purchase of a megaphone or the hiring or construction of a building for church services, or the payment of staff salaries, and other bills; money is needed in spreading the gospel. This has been the greatest challenge for ministers of the gospel of Christ. So many women and men of God are so frustrated with the preaching of the gospel as a result of lack of money. Many have given up on the ministry while others tried some short cuts that brought shame and disgrace to our Lord Jesus Christ. This is an area in which we all need wisdom. It pleases the devil to keep the church in the darkness of ignorance.

In His earthly ministry, our Lord Jesus Christ needed money to pay His tax and those of His disciples. Even though in that particular instance He depended on Peter's skill (fishing) for a supernatural supply, yet He had partners who provided for Him (Luke 8:1-3). Jesus left us an example: He did not rain money down from heaven; He raised partners. He allowed people to partner with Him in the work. He received their lunch pack for a super abundant provision, He preached from their boats when necessary and He allowed Himself to be anointed with oil by one of His converts. At death He allowed a disciple to lay His body in his new tomb. Ministry is all about partnership and covenant.

People who were blessed by Jesus during His earthly ministry were wise enough to partner with Him in ministry. What a privilege God has given us to partner with His ministers in ministry! God's pattern is that the Christian in the market place should make material and financial provision for His work, while the minister focuses on the work of the ministry.

CHAPTER TWO

RULING OVER
THE REALM OF THE AIR

In my view, the air force of any nation is a powerful watchdog. The advantage of the air is that it is above the Sea and the land. From the air you attain a position of dominance and you can view happenings and events that may not be obvious to the eye at ground level. When the battle on the ground becomes tough for the ground force, the air force is called in to clear the way.

The realm of the air is a vantage point in times of battle. In the Old Testament, whenever Israel was in battle, the watchmen stood on the watchtower of the city to view movements and bring reports to the king.

1. RULING WITH CHRIST IN THE HEAVENLIES (GOD'S ABODE)

The heavens are hanging above the air and the third heavens are the abode of God Almighty, which means God rules from the heavens (2 Corinthians 12:2). The scriptures say we are seated in the Heavenly Places with Christ Jesus far above all principalities and powers. What an advantageous position from where to fight our spiritual battles and rule with the Lord Jesus as the Captain of the Lord's Army! We are in a seated position with Him, which means we are fighting from a winning position; we are called to enforce the victory of Christ.

2. RULING OVER THE PRINCE OF THE AIR

The devil is referred to as *"the prince of the power of the air"* (Ephesians 2:2) and the prince of this world (John 12:31; 14:30; 16:11). Most of our battles are fought in the realm of the air – the heavenlies. The air is also the seat of the prince of the air – he works out strategies for his battles from the air.

> *"And you He made alive, who were dead in trespasses and sins, in which you once walked according to the course of this world, according to the prince of the power of the air, the spirit who now works in the sons of disobedience."* Ephesians 2:1-2

> *"Therefore I also, after I heard of your faith in the Lord Jesus and your love for all the saints, do not cease to give thanks for you, making mention of you in my prayers: that God of our Lord Jesus Christ, the Father of glory, may give you the spirit of wisdom and revelation in the knowledge of Him, the eyes of your understanding being enlightened; that you may know what is the hope of His calling, what are the riches of the glory of His inheritance in the saints, and what is the exceeding greatness of His power toward us who believe, according to the working of His mighty power which He worked in Christ when He raised Him from the dead and seated Him at His right hand in the heavenly places, far above all principality and power and might and dominion, and every name that is named, not only in this age but also in that which is to come. And He put all things under His feet, and gave Him to be head over all things to the church, which is His body, the fullness of Him who fills all in all."* Ephesians 1:15-23

3. THE AIRWAVES: A POWERFUL MEDIUM OF COMMUNICATION

I want to illustrate ruling over the air first of all from a spiritual perspective: the realm of spiritual warfare. I also want to stress the importance of taking dominion over the realm of your life and environment through spiritual warfare.

The watchman is always at the tower of a city or nation from where he views events around the city or nation and announces to the king what is approaching. This is similar to the intelligence service of any nation. The fastest medium for covering an entire nation with any information, good or evil, is the AIR. The realm of the air is therefore a very powerful medium of *communication.*

The devil rules from the air – remember, he is called the prince of the air. The first assignment I was engaged in at the beginning of my pastoral work was spiritual warfare. At the time, I did not understand why I had to fight so many battles at that early stage of the work. The spirit of witchcraft was at work, just as in any other ministry, trying to control, manipulate and intimidate. I did not enjoy fighting but I had no choice. I praise God for giving me victory at every stage of the battle! Each victory moved me on to the next level of the ministry.

The devil makes very powerful use of spoken words in the form of blackmail, defamation of character, spells, lies, curses, etc. All these are forms of communication. When such negative utterances are released into one's realm and are allowed to take root, then depression, discouragement, fear, doubt, death, and the like begin to manifest.

Saturate your Realm with the Word of God Daily

As a child of God, it is important for you to speak the Word of God into your realm on a daily basis. Start each day with canceling negative pronouncements of the devil over your life, family and work and exalting the Word of God over your entire realm. Declare that the powers of spells are broken off you and all that belongs to you. Silence the voice of doubt and fear, confusion and destruction in your realm by saying what the Word of God says regarding any given situation in your life. You must recognize that the realm of your thought is the devil's battlefield. Once you learn to defeat him in your thought life, he will go no further with his harassment and manipulations.

> *"For though we walk in the flesh, we do not war according to the flesh. For the weapons of our warfare are not carnal but mighty in God, for pulling down strongholds, casting down* **arguments and every high thing** *that exalts itself against the knowledge of God, bringing* **every thought into captivity** *to the obedience of Christ, and being ready to punish all disobedience when your obedience is fulfilled."* 2 Corinthians 10:3-6

In ruling over the *"birds of the air"* (Genesis 1: 28), the birds Noah sent out of the Ark when the flood began to recede come to mind.

> *"So it came to pass, at the end of forty days, that Noah opened the window of the ark which he had made. Then he sent out a raven, which kept going to and fro until the waters had dried up from the earth. He also sent out from himself a dove, to see if the waters had receded from the face of the ground. But the bird found no resting place for the sole of her foot, and she returned into the ark to him, for the waters were on the face of the whole earth. So he put out his hand and took her, and drew her into the ark to himself. And he waited yet another seven days, and again he sent the dove out from the ark. Then the dove came to him in the evening, and behold, a freshly plucked olive leaf was in her mouth; and Noah knew that the waters had receded from the earth. So he waited yet another seven days and sent out the dove, which did not return again to him anymore."* Genesis 8:6-12

The raven did not return to the Ark after being sent out to assess the degree of the dryness of the ground, probably as a result of the decaying bodies it found for food (the raven is an unclean bird). Noah's sending out the raven on a good mission is like using the seemingly polluted airwaves to propagate and promote the good news of the kingdom of God. When the dove was sent out the second time, it came back with a message – a green olive leaf in its beak. Both birds were powerful agents of *communication*.

In the beautiful nation of Rwanda in East Central Africa, about one million people were killed in a horrifying genocide in 1994. The genocide was perpetrated through the use of the radio – the *airwaves*. Hollywood in America is ruling the world through demonic films unleashed to destroy future generations and family values via the airwaves.

The Almighty God intends for His Church to rule over the airwaves. Putting the gospel on the air should not be seen as showing off a televangelist and his ministry, but as domination of the airwaves for God's Kingdom. The airwaves are the most powerful way to fill the earth with the knowledge of the Lord just as the waters cover the sea! How I pray that every viable ministry in the Church body will be on the air, tearing down the kingdom of darkness and filling the whole earth with the love of Christ.

In *spiritual warfare*, we clean out the atmosphere around us. We *rule* over our environment as we enthrone the Lord Jesus Christ over our atmosphere. Whatever you do - buy a property, move into a rented apartment, start a new business, start a new Church ministry, start a missionary work; wherever you find yourself, take charge of your atmosphere through spiritual warfare. Notice my choice of the term *spiritual warfare* instead of prayer. This is to differentiate between our short, half-hearted prayers and spending quality time in expelling demons from our atmosphere before settling down to business. Prophesy the word of God into that realm.

In *worship*, we enthrone the presence of the Lord God all around us. Moment by moment, on a daily basis, I enjoy the abiding presence of the Lord in my life and home. Our church is a worshipping one and visiting guest ministers always testify of the peace of God around my home, the church and me. I would not trade His presence for anything else in this world! This is because I consciously create a Holy Spirit-filled atmosphere. This does not make me a spiritual fake; I live a normal life, but I am God-conscious most of the time. *"In Him we live and move and have our being*

4. CREATING AN ATMOSPHERE FOR THE MIRACULOUS

Ruling over the birds of the air can also be seen as *creating an atmosphere* for the Holy Spirit of God to move and perform the miraculous. The gifts of the Holy Spirit flourish in such atmospheres.

My divine mandate is to *build a people of worship, power and wealth*. By the grace of God, the Holy Spirit has made me a worshipper and I have witnessed the power of God *in spiritual warfare through worship*. The battles of life made me a worshipper. I have witnessed the healings of breast cancer, cancer of the stomach and deliverance from the spirit of death (several times) while I led worship in our Miracle Services. Just creating an atmosphere for the Holy Spirit to move brings the miraculous into the realm of God's people.

My familiar tools of warfare are the *Word* of God and *worship*. The Holy Spirit gave me great victories in battles through worship. I always take charge of my realm (personal life, family, ministry) in spiritual warfare through worship. In my last book on spiritual warfare *"Fighting the Battles of Life - Deliverance form the Spirit of Witchcraft,* I shared some of the battles I fought in ministry and in my personal life as a result of the idolatrous inheritances from my father's house. Much of my victories came through the act of worshipping the Lord. You need to read that instructive book. I praise God that in all those battles I came out more than a conqueror!

5. CONQUERING THE AIRWAVES THROUGH MEDIA MINISTRY

The fifth dimension in *ruling over the air* is taking the works of your hands on the air (media ministry). In a very practical sense, the Lord intends for His children to exploit to the maximum, the benefits of the media in spreading the gospel of our Lord Jesus Christ.

This also applies to the area of one's secular business.

The first time I began my studies on Genesis 1:28, I felt like reversing the order of arrangement in that verse but then, the Holy Spirit caught my attention. I felt it should read, "*... rule over every living thing that moves on the earth, ...*" first, then sea and air. The Holy Spirit pointed out to me that the scriptures are usually arranged in their order of importance. This is true because you cannot just begin by going on the air or land without money to equip you adequately.

Now, I know that sometimes in ministry it may seem like you may start off without money. For instance, someone may favor you with accommodation without you having to pay rent immediately. The truth of the matter is that the provision of the accommodation did cost the giver some money. In fact, this was exactly how I started my pastoral work, but after a period of grace we began paying rent for the same free accommodation. I believe this is the reason why God starts us off with ruling over the fish of the sea, just to stress its importance in the sphere of life, for money answers all things.

On the assumption that everything you needed to start your vision was given to you freely, know that there should be wisdom as to how to raise money to fund and sustain your vision. Know that you will not go too far before you discover that money is key to your vision. For someone in business, it is obvious that you are in it to make money, so utilize the opportunities available to you through the media and market your products. Little wonder the Bible says, "*money answers everything*" (Ecclesiastes 10:19).

Remember that the air places you in a position of dominance.

In these times when it is becoming more difficult to take the gospel of the Kingdom to "closed" nations, especially in the 10/40 Window of the world, the media ministry becomes a very powerful and relevant tool for the spread of that message. Information technology is said to have turned the world into a global village. Man has truly subdued "the birds of the air." Information today travels at the speed of light.

Church ministries and Christian-owned secular businesses came to the limelight through the media after being in obscurity.

The Lord indeed wants you to use this medium to conquer the world. Three years after I founded the Logos Aflame Ministries, we went on the air, and were there for over two years. Little did I know that the Lord used those years to announce my presence to my nation. The impact of those few years is still felt today. These days as I travel, I meet people in foreign countries that came to know the Lord through my media ministry.

You may have the most anointed ministry on earth meant to affect many nations, but ignorance of the vantage position of the media ministry will keep you in obscurity. Often, one hears ignorant people with misconstrued ideas of media ministry say that the televangelists are on the air to promote themselves. "Jesus never promoted Himself," they say. Do not allow such religious talks to keep you from maximizing the power of the media. Change your strategy today. Position the work in your hands in a place of dominance!

You can penetrate people's homes and minds through the radio, television, the internet, billboards, print media, various forms of literature, audio and video tapes, compact discs and the like. The world uses the entire media to invade people's lives, most times with corrupt and highly demonic activities. Let's get in there and counter the hellish activities with the gospel of hope in Christ Jesus.

6. THE WIND

Prophetically, the wind in the Bible is a powerful instrument in God's hand to accomplish His purposes. In Exodus 10:13, 19-20, the eighth judgment on Egypt was the plague of locusts which was brought about by the wind of the Lord: *"So Moses stretched out his rod over the land of Egypt, and the Lord brought an **east wind** on the land all that night. When it was morning, the **east wind** brought the locusts ... And the Lord turned a very strong west wind, which took the locusts away and blew them into the Red Sea. There remained not one locust in all the territory of Egypt."*

Also, in Exodus 14:21-22 at the Red Sea, during the Exodus of Israel from Egypt, God employed the services of the East Wind which traveled all night to drive back the waters that formed walls on the two sides of the sea and Israel crossed on dry ground: *"Then Moses stretched out his hand over the sea; and the Lord caused the* *sea to go back by a strong **east wind** all night, and made the sea into dry land, and the waters were divided. So the children of Israel went into the midst of the sea on the dry ground, and the waters were a wall to their right hand and on their left."*

Another example occurs in the valley of dry bones in Ezekiel 37:9: *"Then said he unto me, Prophesy unto the wind, prophesy, son of man, and say to the wind, Thus saith the LORD God: Come from the four winds, O breath, and breathe upon these slain, that they may live."* In this passage, the wind brought life to a dead situation. The gospel, preached through the airwaves sends the Good News to obscure corners of the earth, where we may never get to in person. Dead situations in a person's life come alive when the Holy Spirit is invited to breathe on them! Romans 8:11 says, *"But if the Spirit of Him who raised Jesus from the dead dwells in you, He who raised Christ from the dead will also give life to your mortal bodies through His Spirit who dwells in you."*

Acts of the Apostles 2:1-4 tells us *"When the Day of Pentecost had fully come, they were all with one accord in one place. And suddenly there came a sound from heaven, as of a rushing mighty wind, and it filled the whole house where they were sitting. Then there appeared to them divided tongues, as of fire, and one sat upon each of them. And they were all filled with the Holy Spirit and began to speak with other tongues, as the Spirit gave them utterance."* Here, the coming of the Holy Spirit is depicted as "a rushing mighty wind." I often call on the wind of the Holy Spirit in battle, and at other times I call on Him to blow in His wind of peace and restoration.

7. FINANCING A LIE AT CHRIST'S RESURRECTION

At the resurrection of Christ, the Roman soldiers reported His resurrection to the religious leaders who had been responsible for His death. The soldiers were afraid to report to their superiors, as training required that they be put to death in place of any convict that escaped from their custody. Afraid of the death penalty, they reported the mystery of Christ's resurrection to the religious leaders instead of to their superiors.

The religious leaders then promised to cover up the failure of the soldiers to keep Christ in the tomb as planned by financing a lie that the disciples of Jesus stole His body while the soldiers slept. This is still going on today as religious leaders are financing wrong teachings on the air. Worst of all, the devil finances all manners of lies against the gospel today. Hollywood can finance a film to the tune of 200 million dollars to promote homosexual, violent or promiscuous lifestyles, all of which oppose the Word of God. This is why the Church needs to understand her place in ruling in dominion over the airwaves. More Christians should work towards preaching the gospel through film-making as with Mel Gibson's *The Passion of The Christ*, the *Jesus* film of Bill Bright and others.

The preaching of the gospel today through the film industry is like Christ's parables to the world. Jesus spoke to the world through parables thereby creating inquisitiveness in them to search for the real meaning of what he said. He did however explain the same parables to His disciples (the Church). The present generation *hears* through their *sight* and *sees* through their *ears*. Therefore in order to reach them, the gospel must be presented in their language! Enough of allowing the devil to finance his lies through the airwaves!

CHAPTER THREE

RULING OVER THE LAND

The third realm of rulership is the *land*. In Genesis 3, God placed a curse on the land because of the sin of Adam, the first man. Of the three realms of dominion, the land possesses more challenges because it is man's physical place of abode. The activities in the other two realms of rulership are ultimately focused on the land. When money is made through the sea (commerce) and the airwaves are invaded, the results of the two realms rest on the land, whether blessings or curses. Another reason the land poses many challenges is that God cursed the land because of Adam's sin. Yet, God's original instruction to man concerning the land was to *occupy*. Adam was to tend the Garden of Eden and multiply himself through procreation and fill the earth. It is noteworthy that man regained what he lost through the death and resurrection of Jesus Christ. Jesus Christ has replace the curse on the ground with His blessing.

There are basic principles involved in ruling over the land. The first man on earth was created and put in the Garden of Eden to occupy the land. God's promise to Abraham was to give him a land to occupy. Land is very significant in the existence of man on earth. Ownership of land perpetuates your name on earth. In Africa, land matters have sent millions of people to early graves. In the civilized nations, land matters are handled differently.

Occupying the land from a scriptural perspective requires following God's directions strictly in strategic warfare. We shall examine this in the journey of Israel from Egypt to Canaan: In Genesis 12:1-3, God commanded Abraham to leave his country, family and his father's house and to go to a land He would show him. By Genesis 13, Abraham was already in Canaan. Four generations away from him, his great grand children returned to Egypt and stayed there for 430 years until Moses showed up to deliver them from slavery. God started them on a new journey from Egypt, back to His promised land for them. It took several battles and over 40 years for Israel to occupy that Promised Land.

On the eve of Israel's departure from Egypt, they went into a covenant relationship with God as they slaughtered the Passover lambs. It is important to note that God demanded a sacrifice before they could depart from the land of their enemies in preparation for the journey to His promised land for them. It is pertinent to note that:

– The Passover in Egypt gave Israel adequate assurances of God's ability not only to deliver them from their strong enemies but also of His faithfulness in bringing them into their Promised Land.
– The Passover Sacrifice was a shadow of the blood of Jesus and pointed to the fact that Christ's blood is the ultimate sacrifice required for access into God's covenant promises for us now and for the future.
– Breaking the original curse on the land will require cutting a covenant with the Lord. By this I mean atoning for the redemption of the particular land by the blood of Jesus Christ and by cutting a fresh covenant with God with your money – seed.

We shall take a closer look at our covenant relationship with God in chapter 5.

Moses, the servant of God, was given the mandate to lead Israel out of Egypt to the land of Canaan. However, when he missed God on the occasion of striking the rock instead of speaking to it, he was denied entry into Canaan by God Himself (Numbers 20:3-13). After Moses' demise, Joshua, his minister, was given the assignment to take the people of Israel into the Promised Land and to divide the land among the tribes of Israel.

Principles Guiding Occupation of land

1. *YOUR MONEY—SEED IS REQUIRED AS SACRIFICE FOR THE REDEMPTION OF YOUR LAND.*

The final battle to possess the land of Canaan began with the Passover sacrifice in Egypt:

> *"Now the LORD spoke to Moses and Aaron in the land of Egypt, saying, "This month shall be your beginning of months; it shall be the first month of the year to you. Speak to all the congregation of Israel, saying: 'On the tenth of this month every man shall take for himself a lamb, according to the house of his father, a lamb for a household."* Exodus 12:1-3

> *"And thus you shall eat it in: with a belt on your waist, your sandals on your feet, and your staff in your hand. So you shall eat it in haste. It is the LORD's Passover. For I will pass through the land of Egypt on that night, and will strike all the first-born in the land of Egypt, both man and beast; and against all the gods of Egypt I will execute judge-ment: I am the LORD. Now the blood shall be a sign for you on the houses where you are. And when I see the blood, I will pass over you; and the plague shall not be on you to destroy you when I strike the land of Egypt"* Exodus 12:11-13

> *And it came to pass at midnight that the LORD struck all the firstborn in the land of Egypt, from the firstborn of Pharaoh who sat on his throne to the firstborn of the captive who was in the dungeon, and all the firstborn of livestock. So Pharaoh rose in the*

night, he, all his servants, and all the Egyptians; and there was a great cry in Egypt, for there was not a house where there was not one dead. Then he called for Moses and Aaron by night, and said, "Rise, go out from among my people, both you and the children of Israel. And go, serve the LORD as you have said. And take your flocks and your herds, as you have said, and be gone: and bless me also." And the Egyptians urged the people, that they might send them out of the land in haste. For they said, "We shall all be dead." So the people took their dough before it was leavened, having their kneading bowls bound up in their clothes on their shoulders. Now the children of Israel had done according to the word of Moses, and they had asked from the Egyptians articles of silver, articles of gold, and clothing. And the LORD had given the people favor in the sight of the Egyptians, so that they granted them what they requested. Thus they plundered the Egyptians." Exodus 12:29-36

The land of Egypt had held the children of Israel in captivity for 430 years. Their stay in Egypt began with honor during the lifetime of Joseph and degenerated to a life of slavery after the death of Joseph, when a Pharaoh who did not know Joseph came to the throne of Egypt. At God's appointed time, He sent Moses to deliver His people from the land but not without a protracted battle, for the gods of the land of Egypt would not let them go. God performed 10 signs and wonders in order to display His power over the powers of the gods of the land, yet the gods remained adamant. God instructed Israel through Moses to cut a special covenant with Him, renewing the covenant He made with Abraham their forefather. It was only after the Passover covenant sacrifice had been cut and God had dealt the final blow to the gods of the land that Pharaoh was ready to release the Israelites from Egypt. We really need to give God time to deal with enemies on our behalf. Sometimes the battle is so fierce that we tend to give up fighting. The passage of time enables God to process our maturity and depth in Him.

This reminds me of the battle we fought over a particular piece of real estate (over 2 acres of land) that the Lord gave us for ministry work. Unknown to me, this property was a beehive of demonic activities because the previous owner was a member of the Rosicrucian Order. We fought life-threatening battles on this property. At the beginning of the battles, I had little knowledge about redeeming the land by ratifying my covenant with the Lord with my money-seed (my offerings). We fasted, prayed and did a lot of spiritual warfare. It seemed like the more we prayed the more intense the battle became.

Three years into our stay on the property, the entire flock was scattered. A congregation of almost 1,000 people decreased to about 20 people within 12 months. At a point we took the matter before the Lord at the Holy Communion table, but it was not until 9 years later that the demonic hold on the land was finally broken when I learnt about cutting covenant with the Lord with my money-seed! I sowed several thousands of dollars into Dr. Mike Murdock's ministries as the Lord led me. This whole battle had plunged me into a crippling depression that lasted 7 years. Towards the end of the 7th year of this depression, the Lord placed one of Dr. Mike Murdock's books, "The Leadership Secrets of Jesus Christ" into my hands as a birthday gift from one of my precious church leaders, Akolisa Ekwueme. God bless his kind heart. This book instantly set me free from this terrible depression.

Your money should be involved in the deliverance of your landed property. Our sacrifices to the Lord today are in the form of our offerings and not animal sacrifices. Sow money-seeds as a ratification of your covenant with the Lord.

2. DISPOSSESSING THE ENEMY BEFORE POSSESSING THE LAND.

"Now the LORD spoke to Moses in the plains of Moab by the Jordan, saying "Speak to the children of Israel and say to them: 'When you have crossed

the Jordan into the land of Canaan, then **you shall drive out all the inhabitants of the land from before you, destroy all their engraved stones, destroy all their molded images, and demolish all their high places; you shall dispossess the inhabitants of the land and dwell in it, for I have given you the land to possess.** *And you shall divide the land by lot as an inheritance among your families; to the larger you shall give the larger inheritance, and to the smaller you shall give the smaller inheritance; there everyone's inheritance shall be whatever falls to him by lot. You shall inherit according to the tribes of your fathers. But if you do not drive out the inhabitants of the land from before you, then it shall be that those whom you let remain shall be irritants in your eyes and thorns in your sides, and they shall harass you in the land where you dwell. Moreover it shall be that I will do to you as I thought to do to them'."*
Numbers 33:50-56

Canaan was already occupied by the Canaanites before the Lord gave His promise to Abraham. His intention was for Israel to dispossess the occupants of the land before they could occupy it. The occupants of the land of Canaan were idolaters who rejected the God of the land, and chose instead to worship the creatures instead of the Creator. For this reason, God gave their land over to Israel. Israel had to fight battles every inch of the way, but not without the help of the Lord their God. Consider each of the blessings the Lord has given you and see how many battles you had to fight to possess and maintain them. It could be your marriage, children, the works of your hands, property, finances, etc. My counseling sessions with people reveal the levels of warfare that go on in families to maintain their covenant to remain together as one unit. Parents fight so many battles to rescue their children from the clutches of the devil.

Defeating the Principalities

Every landed property given to our ministry by the Lord had to be possessed through much battle in spiritual warfare. It took 12 months of delay to possess the first place of worship we rented. I could not figure out what the delay was all about. At first, the property was offered to us free but we could never get in there without a fight. It took much prayer and negotiations before the keys were released to us and we ended up paying rent in place of the initial free offer.

Three years into our stay on that property, the Lord opened up the realm of that community and I saw the demonic principality in charge of that particular community. It is difficult to describe its form, but it was a huge, towering creature that looked more like a 10-foot tall robot. His footsteps shook the ground as he advanced towards me. He had some smaller demons hanging around him, ready to obey his commands. The principality came charging at me, complaining that I had been disturbing his peace in the community. He ordered me to cease my activities. Then he invited me to an open fight with him. His little demons hailed him as he issued his threats. In that vision I was scared to face him but I saw our intercessors saying to me, "Pastor go after him. You are able to face him." When the principality saw that we were not compromising, and when he saw the bright and glorious light surrounding me, he made a shift in his stance and began to seek a compromise with me.

The history behind that community was that nothing ever succeeded in that environment. Businesses constantly moved in and out of the neighborhood and there were frequent armed robberies resulting in deaths. But as we moved into the community, we began to take possession through much prayer and fasting, expelling the demons operating in the community and cleaning out that realm in the name of Jesus and by His Blood, and of course, with the Word of God as our sword. This was what the principality was referring to as "disturbance." Praise God for the Holy Spirit, the Revealer of Truth! I witnessed the most miraculous manifestations of the gifts of the Holy Spirit through my life in the five years we were on that property. Now, ten years later, when I drive through the community, I am constantly amazed at the level of development there. The church truly is the Light of the world. Our presence in that community brought progress there, and even after we moved on to another place, the light of the Lord remained there. Hallelujah!

We rented that property for five years before the Lord gave us a warehouse in another part of the city, which we bought and renovated. We moved into this new property with a 7-day fast and prayer. On the third day of the fast, the principality of that community appeared to me and raised a bitter complaint against me, asking me what he had done to me that caused me to give him so much trouble. He told me that he was going to disturb me just as I had disturbed him. On the day following this encounter, we suffered a frustrating traffic jam in the entire area and members of our congregation were unable to get to the church for the corporate prayers to round up that day's fast. On the fifth day, when we met in church, people told of their frustrations in the terrible traffic of the previous day. This was just the beginning of my battles on this property.

I fought so many life-threatening battles on this particular property, both with the landowner (who constantly took us to law court) and with the government as I refused to give bribes to officials to get our papers. It took six years to process the government papers for the approval of the land. The crowning battle was when the spirit of witchcraft invaded the congregation. Some of my leaders began clamoring for positions and the fight became internal. This was the worst and most dangerous of all the battles I had fought. I almost gave up on the ministry at that point. The wound from that internal battle festered until the Lord Jesus intervened and healed me. It took almost 8 years for me to receive healing from the Lord over those internal battles. I declined into depression. I praise God that the battle was won at last! *(Read the first point under principles guiding occupation of land)*

This area of the city of Lagos – Agidingbi, Ikeja – was a well-known danger zone. Several killings by armed bandits occurred there on a daily basis in those late 1980s and early 1990s. Several landlords moved out of their buildings after one or two attempts on their lives. There were constant reports of murders in the area. At the end of our street was a huge refuse dump. It was literarily an abandoned area. One day I asked the Lord what to do about the safety of some of my staff who lived on the church premises and the Lord said that I should bring them to Him in covenant at the Holy Communion table. So I served them the Holy Communion declaring that there would be no death on that premises, and it has been so. At the time of writing this book, we have been on that property for over 14 years with no evil report. Was it really the Lord who gave us that property that almost took my life? Yes! The Lord gave me this place when I desperately needed to relocate the church. I testify to the glory of our great God that some of the most powerful miracles in my ministry were witnessed on that property. I witnessed the healing of breast cancer and several deliverances from death. This was the most prosperous time of my work in the ministry numerically, in the quality of membership and financially. Today, over 14 years later, that community of death has become a thriving business district in the city.

While the battle on the second land lasted, the Lord graciously gave us another property in a different location in the city, at Lekki Peninsula. This third property was given to us by a precious and dear couple, Ambassador Victor and Dr. Victoria Taylor, and presently houses our head office. I can say that the other properties were blessings from the Lord, but this third property became like our Rehoboth. God indeed made room for us! We did fight battles here but not of the magnitude in the first two places.

3. INVOLVEMENT OF SPIRITUAL LEADERS INVITES THE PRESENCE OF GOD

> *"These are the names of the men who shall divide the land among you as an inheritance: Eleazar the priest and Joshua son of Nun."* Numbers 34:17

We saw earlier that God cursed the land as a result of the sin of the first man Adam. Curses also come as a result of breaking a covenant. This calls for us as believers to always dedicate whatever property we own or occupy. This must include money-seed as offerings for the dedication of the land to break the original curse placed on it by God in the Garden of Eden.

Secondly, believers living in idolatrous nations must break demonic covenants over the land, some of which have lasted several generations. In such nations, some families that are involved in the occult dedicate parcels of their family lands to the devil with animal blood and sometimes with human blood. When other people subsequently purchase such land or buildings or businesses without destroying the demonic covenants and establishing a new covenant in the name of the Lord, they fight the battles of their lives.

Some years back, a family in our church moved into a beautiful apartment. One day they came to me requesting for prayers over the property, as there were strange movements within the house. They heard strange voices and objects were falling off the wall. This might have been as a result of some demonic dedications on the property by the landowner or the previous tenant.

The Call of Gideon in the book of Judges 6 teaches a vital lesson on the importance of demolishing demonic altars in order to raise a new one in the name of the Lord. Involve your spiritual leader (your pastor) in the dedication of land and other material blessings unto the Lord. There should be a tangible offering upon the altar of that dedication. Your offering ratifies your covenant with God on that property. The second church property mentioned earlier posed so many challenges that I had to sow so much money-seed for the deliverance of that land.

In Numbers 35:6-8, God instructed Israel through Moses, saying, *"Now among the cities which you will give to the Levites you shall appoint six cities of refuge, to which a manslayer may flee. And to these you shall add forty-two cities. So all the cities you will give to the Levites shall be forty-eight; these you shall give with their common-land. And the cities which you will give shall be from the possession of the children of Israel; from the larger tribe you shall give many, from the smaller you shall give few. Each shall give some of its cities to the Levites, in proportion to the inheritance that each receives."*

God, in this passage, wanted Israel to willingly involve the Levites in their landed possessions. Your pastor represents God's spiritual authority over your life. God's ministers should be treated as covenant partners in God's kingdom. God told Israel they were to provide for the Levites among them from their own possessions. And the Levites were to live among the people and not to isolate themselves. Their presence among the people represented God's presence in their midst. When you purchase land or other properties, you should give a tangible covenant seed on the property and let your minister dedicate it for you.

4. WALKING IN OBEDIENCE TO GOD'S WORD

Our covenant-keeping God will never fail in His promises. He promises to protect and keep you in the land if only you can walk in obedience to Him. Do the best you can to walk in love with the Lord. True love for the Lord will keep you from deliberate disobedience to Him.

> *"Then it shall come to pass, because you listen to these judgments, and keep and do them, that the LORD your God will keep with you the covenant and the mercy which He swore to your fathers. And He will love you and bless you and multiply you; He will also bless the fruit of your womb and the fruit of your land, your grain and your new wine and your oil, the increase of your cattle and the offspring of your flock, in the land of which He swore to your fathers to give you. You shall be blessed above all peoples; there shall not be a male or female barren among you or among your livestock. And the LORD will take away from you all sicknesses, and will afflict you with none of the terrible diseases of Egypt which you have known, but will lay them on those who hate you. Also you shall destroy all the peoples whom the LORD your God delivers over to you; your eyes shall have no pity on them; nor shall you serve their gods, for that will be a snare to you. If you should say in your heart, 'These nations are greater than I; how can I dispossess them?'—you shall not be afraid of them, but you shall remember well what the LORD your God did to Pharaoh and*

to all Egypt: the great trials which your eyes saw, the signs and the wonders, the mighty hand and the outstretched arm, by which the LORD your God brought you out. So shall the Lord your God do to all the peoples of whom you are afraid. Moreover the LORD your God will send the hornet among them until those who are left, who hide themselves from you, are destroyed. You shall not be terrified of them; for the Lord your God, the great and awesome God, is among you. And the Lord your God will drive out those nations before you little by little; you will be unable to destroy them at once, lest the beasts of the field become too numerous for you. But the LORD your God will deliver them over to you, and will inflict defeat upon them until they are destroyed." Deuteronomy 7: 12-24

Obeying God's word and honoring Him on the land and in other blessings He has given you will keep His favor on you and on generations of your children yet unborn.

5. *AVOIDING IDOLATROUS PRACTICES ON YOUR PROMISED LAND*

The primary reason why God allowed the enemies of Israel to come against them was because of the sin of idolatry. Many nations of the world, especially the idolatrous ones, are thrown out of their land; the land seems to vomit them out. Generations of their children live outside their native countries. Whenever the people of Israel abandoned the Lord and worshipped other gods, God stirred up their enemies to fight against them and defeat them. If they remained in their sins, the land spewed them out and God gave the land a Sabbath rest.

"And it shall be that just as the LORD rejoiced over you to do you good and multiply you, so the LORD will rejoice over you to destroy you and bring you to nothing; and you shall be plucked from off the land

which you go to possess. Then the LORD will scatter
you among all the peoples, from one end of the earth
to the other, and there you shall serve other gods,
which neither you nor your fathers have known –
wood and stone. And among those nations you shall
find no rest, nor shall the sole of your foot have a
resting place; but there the LORD will give you a
trembling heart, failing eyes, and anguish of soul.

Your life shall hang in doubt before you; you
shall fear day and night, and have no assurance of
life. In the morning you shall say, 'Oh, that it were
evening!' And at evening you shall say, 'Oh, that it
were morning!' because of the fear which terrifies
your heart, and because of the sight which your eyes
see." Deuteronomy 28: 63-67

In some cases the Lord's judgment comes in the form of inva-
sion of the land by your enemies. As individuals, when our object
of worship is shifted from the Lord to other things, our lives will be
invaded by all kinds of attacks from the enemy. We must watch out
for idolatrous practices or covetousness and avoid them.

6. *REMOVAL OF LAND MARKS*

"Cursed is the one who removes his neighbor's
landmark." Deuteronomy 27:17

Removal of landmarks has wiped away entire communities.
This principle requires that we live uprightly with our fellow men.
Righteous living is a powerful weapon of spiritual warfare: It shall
establish you in the land.

SECTION ONE

God gave the earth (sea, air and land) to humans to subdue and rule. The earth is man's domain.

The three realms of rulership are being conquered by the world on daily basis; scientists work hard to make new discoveries on how to rule the air. New and more modern aircrafts are produced to dominate the air. Astronauts are not satisfied with their visits to the moon; they are exploring the possibilities of making a home for human beings there.

The Internet is used for treading across the globe. It is no longer business as usual. Business is now made easier in transaction and delivery to any part of the globe. There is a ruling over the sea.

Mineral resources underneath the ground are making the world richer. Real Estate is thieving in different parts of the globe.

God laid down principles in His word that will enable us occupy and rule over the land. Nations founded on idolatrous practices has given the devil a legal hold to their land. Think about the people of Israel in the land of Egypt for 430 years; the gods of Egypt would not let them go not until Israel cut the Passover Covenant with God.

Whenever apiece of property is purchased or rented there is need to raise an altar with money seed, as a dedication offering to the Lord.

Businesses bought from others should be dedicated to the Lord as an altar is raised with money seed.

Involvement of spiritual leaders (Pastors) in such dedications are proper and Scriptural.

In all of these the Church body is yet to understand her divine mandate to conquer these three realms. Once the Church understands that her Lord has given her the world to conquer and go about it His way, ministry will take a different dimension on earth. May that day come when there will be more wealth in the Church than we see today.

SECTION TWO

Discover how to rule over wealth by applying the principles of God's Word in the Bible.

CHAPTER FOUR

THE ORIGIN OF WEALTH—GOD OR SATAN?

Wealth is not just money. Wealth has to do primarily with *who you are* before considering possessions, money or riches. Wealth begins *within you*. Wealth is also influence, connections and your sphere of power. Where else can we search for the source of true wealth, but from the Book of Beginnings – the Bible?

Much of our successes and failures in life begin in our minds. The book of Proverbs 23:7 says, *"For as he thinks in his heart, so is he."* Yes, as a man thinks so he is. You may have been born poor but have always seen yourself as a wealthy person, having a mindset to make it in life: there your journey to wealth creation begins. Your mindset determines the direction you face in life and becomes the driving force that propels you to soar above any obstacle. A palace does not make a king; and a palace without a king is no kingdom. It is the king that adds honor and dignity to the palace.

Wealth begins in your mind!

This is why the unsaved prosper once they embrace the principles of wealth creation. The principles of sowing and reaping work for the saved as well as the unsaved alike; it is the one who obeys the rules of sowing that harvests. For this reason you must re-examine and contrast your "religious beliefs" against this very topic of *wealth*, in the light of the teachings of the Bible. Too much garbage in the mind will obstruct the illumination of the truth. Apostle Paul in Romans 12:2 admonishes us " *...not to conform to the patterns of this world, but be transformed by the renewing of your mind. Then you will be able to test and prove what God's will is—His good, pleasing and perfect will." (NIV)*

The most powerful tool for renewing our minds is the Bible – the Word of God. Religion teaches us that poverty is synonymous with righteousness. One often hears religious people paint a horrible picture of a *poor* Jesus, who was always found with the poor. It often sounds as if Jesus had nothing but condemnation for the rich because of their riches. For many years I heard preachers use this passage of the Bible to buttress their belief that the rich will not enter God's kingdom; *"Then Jesus looked around and said to His disciples, 'How hard it is for those who have riches to enter the kingdom of God!"* But read the next verse, *"And the disciples were astonished at His words. But Jesus answered again and said to them, 'Children, how hard it is for those who <u>trust</u> in riches to enter the kingdom of God! It is easier for a camel to go through the eye of a needle than for a rich man to enter the kingdom of God."* Mark 10:23-25.

I believe the emphasis here is on the words **"trust in"** and not the possession of riches. Some make it look like the Lord never showed interest in the good things of this life. In this particular instant the young rich ruler is possessed by his possessions. That is the crux of the matter.

Jesus and the Wealthy

Several passages in the Bible demonstrate that Jesus honored invitations to be with some of the prominent people of His time:

    a. He was with Zacchaeus in Luke 19:2-10: *"Now behold, there was a man named Zacchaeus who was a chief tax collector, and was rich. And he sought to see who Jesus was, but could not because of the crowd, for he was of short stature. So he ran and climbed up into a sycamore tree to see Him, for he was going to pass that way. And when Jesus came to the place, he looked up and saw him, and said to him, "Zacchaeus, make haste and come down, for today I must stay at your house." So he made haste and came down, and received Him joyfully. But when they saw it, they all complained, saying, "He has gone to be a guest with a man who is a sinner." Then Zacchaeus stood and said to the Lord, "Look, Lord, I give half of my goods to the poor; and if I have taken anything from anyone by false accusation, I restore fourfold." And Jesus said to him, "Today salvation has come to this house, because he also is a son of Abraham; for the son of Man has come to seek and to save that which was lost."*

b. He honored Simon the leper's invitation to a lunch in Luke 7:36; *"Then one of the Pharisees asked Him to eat with him. And He went to the Pharisee's house, and sat down to eat."*

c. His relationship with Nicodemus, one of the prominent religious leaders of His time, is recorded in the book of John: *"There was a man of the Pharisees named Nicodemus, a ruler of the Jews. This man cane to Jesus by night and said to Him, "Rabbi, we know that You are a teacher come from God; for no one can do these signs that You do unless God is with him."* (John 3:1-2); *"Nicodemus (he who came to Jesus by night, being one of them) said to them, "Does our law judge a man before it hears him and knows what he is doing?"* (John 7:50-51);

"And Nicodemus, who at first came to Jesus by night, also came, bringing a mixture of myrrh and aloes, about a hundred pounds. Then they took the body of Jesus ..." (John 19:39).

d. Joseph of Arimathea was a respectable figure who requested for the body of Jesus for burial. In John 19:38-42, he buried the body of Jesus in his personal tomb: *"After this, Joseph of Arimathea, being a disciple of Jesus, but secretly, for fear of the Jews, asked Pilate that he might take away the body of Jesus; and Pilate gave him permission. So he came and took the body of Jesus. And Nicodemus, who at first came to Jesus by night, also came, bringing a mixture of myrrh and aloes, about a hundred pounds. Then they took the body of Jesus, and bound it in strips of linen with the spices, as the custom of the Jews is to bury. Now in the place where He was cruci-fied there was a new tomb in which no one had yet been laid. So there they laid Jesus, because of the Jews' Preparation Day, for the tomb was nearby."* Could a poor man own a personal tomb in his lifetime? You must be very wealthy to own a personal tomb while alive. These men in these bible passages were followers of Jesus. Jesus was aware of their wealth and did not reject them as some today would wish. He knew their wealth will someday be needed for His services.

There are more passages in the Bible that show that the good God who made this beautiful earth, is a rich and wealthy Designer and is not in any way against His people handling riches and wealth.

Pour out the old wine of religious beliefs and clean out the old wine skin so it can hold the new wine of the unadulterated Word of God! How important it is to study the Word of God for yourself and discover His mind. All the religious beliefs people carry about are myths that have been communicated from one generation to another; these myths do not replace the word of God. The devil keeps the church ignorant and in poverty in order to slow down, and in many cases, hinders the preaching of the gospel of Jesus Christ.

In the book of Genesis chapters 1 through 3, we see the begin-ning of God's creations. God created everything in abundance with a touch of excellence and beauty. In chapter 2:28, God gave man (man and woman or 'them'), authority to rule over His creation.

In my first book in this wealth creation series, *Living in God's Abundance - A Lifestyle*, I gave the meaning of Eden, as **riches, abundance and delight.** Gen. 2:10-12 also shows that God planted a lot of precious stones and mineral resources in Eden. History tells us that Eden must have been situated in the region of Iraq of today, in the Middle East, and we are aware of the wealth of oil and other mineral resources in that region. *"Now a river went out of Eden to* *water the garden, and from there it parted and became four river-heads. The name of the first is Pishon; it is the one which skirts the whole land of Havilah, where there is gold. And the gold of that land is good. Bdellium and the onyx stone are there."*

The devil did not create wealth; God did. And God did not create anything (wealth inclusive) for the devil and his followers. Think about the lies you may have believed about wealth belonging to the god of mammon or to the marine spirit. The devil may claim to have a hold on wealth, as he made a boast to Jesus on the Mount of Temptation. That claim was as a result of what took place after the fall of man in the book of Genesis when Adam sold out his birthright to the devil, thereby selling out the entire human race. But in the beginning it was not so and Jesus has redeemed and restored man to his original state through His death on the cross. One of the major principles you will learn in this book is that our relationship with God exists by covenant (through the death of Christ on the Cross) and that relationship shall be sustained by the daily sacrifices of our lives, our financial and material offerings to Him, and also through partaking in the Holy Communion.

WHAT THE BIBLE SAYS ABOUT WEALTH

"The Lord makes poor and makes rich; He brings low and He lifts up." I Samuel 2:7 (Amplified Bible)

"And you shall remember the LORD your God, for it is He who gives you power to get wealth, that He may establish His covenant which He swore to your fathers, as it is this day." Deuteronomy 8:18

"The blessing of the Lord makes one rich, and He adds no sorrow with it." Proverbs 10:22

"As for every man to whom God has given riches and wealth, and given him power to eat of it, to receive his heritage and rejoice in his labor - this is the gift of God." Ecclesiastes 5:19

"Yours, O Lord, is the greatness, the power and the glory, the victory and the majesty; for all that is in heaven and in the earth is yours; Yours is the kingdom, O LORD, and You are exalted as head over all. Both riches and honor come from You and You reign over all. In Your hand is power and might; in Your hand it is to make great and to give strength to all."
1 Chronicles 29:11-12

Who gave King Solomon his wealth?

"Then God said to Solomon: 'Because this was in your heart, and you have not asked for riches or wealth or honor or the life of your enemies, nor have asked long life – but have asked wisdom and knowledge for yourself, that you may judge My people over whom I have made you king – wisdom and knowledge are granted to you; and I will give riches and wealth and honor, such as none of the kings have had who were before you, nor shall any after you have the like'." 2 Chronicles 1:11-12

The last two passages above speak not only of riches and wealth but also of exaltation and honor. Many Christians have convinced themselves that our faith in Christ is meant to depict sufferings only and has nothing to do with material blessings or honor and they vehemently come against anyone who believes otherwise.

The Lord Jesus also taught vital lessons on money in the New Testament

The parable of the unjust steward (Luke 16:1-13):

"So the master commended the unjust steward because he had dealt shrewdly. For the sons of this world are more shrewd in their generation than the sons of light. And I say to you, make friends for

*yourselves by unrighteous mammon, that when you
fail, they may receive you into an everlasting home."*
Luke 16:8-9

It is amazing that the Lord Jesus would draw such an analogy in
the above verses concerning the wisdom with which the world
manages money and how His children respond to money.

Lessons from the unfaithful manager:

a. The shrewdness of the unfaithful manager:
b. He knew how to handle failure – he did not give room to
   depression as a result of his failure. Instead;
c. He employed the power of foresight. In order to preserve his
   future, he made friends with the power of money.

Proverbs 18:16 says, *"A man's gift makes room for him, and
brings him before great men"*
Money has the power of attraction, both for good and evil.
Money can unlock some healthy relationships that will unlock other
golden gates for you. Yours could be a purchased gift or it could be
sponsorship for someone's education. Such seeds leave your
present life and go into your future, where you will eventually reap
the harvest.

The Parable of the Hidden Treasure:

*Again the kingdom of heaven is like treasure hidden
in a field, which a man found and hid; and for joy
over it he goes and sells all that he has and buys that
field.* Matthew 13:44

This parable of Jesus is about money. I have heard many
preachers interpret this as someone who found salvation and sold
all he had to purchase it. It is obvious that the Lord Jesus was teaching about the principles of investment. It definitely has a spiritual
dimension to it also.

The Parable of the Pearl of Great Price:

> *"Again, the kingdom of heaven is like a merchant seeking beautiful pearls, who, when he had found one of great price, went and sold all that he had and bought it."* Matthew 13:45

This parable sounds like the last. Jesus again compares the kingdom of heaven with the principles that guide the business world. If He were against wealth then He would have not sighted monetary examples on spiritual matters.

God's Ultimate Purpose for Wealth

> *"And you shall remember the LORD your God, for it is He who gives you power to get wealth, that He may establish His covenant which He swore to your fathers, as it is this day."* Deuteronomy 8:18

1. God's ultimate purpose in wealth creation is that He will establish His covenant of prosperity and wealth with His people, so they can declare His glory on earth. God has given humans the earth as their domain, He has limited Himself by the laws that rule man's domain. God does nothing in man's domain without his cooperation, this is where covenant between God and man becomes the basis for man's success and prosperity.
2. Man must recognize God as the Source of his wealth and prosperity. *"...remember the Lord..."*
3. God desires to *establish* His covenant through His Church. It takes two to make a covenant, and God needs the cooperation of man for this covenant relationship to be established.
4. God establishes His covenant of wealth for the deliverance of mankind as seen in the case of Abraham and Lot:

> *"Now when Abram heard that his brother was taken captive, he armed his three hundred and eighteen*

trained servants who were born in his own house, and went in pursuit as far as Dan. He divided his forces against them by night, and he and his servants attacked them and pursued them as far as Hobah, which is north of Damascus. So he brought back all the goods, and also brought back his brother Lot and his goods, as well as the women and the people." Genesis 14:14-16

What poor man could own 318 personal security guards? Obviously Abraham's wealth was handy for the deliverance of Lot and his household in the time of trouble. In our world today, this could represent some form of social work in our communities that call for the attention of the individual members of the Body of Christ. In many parts of Africa and other parts of the world, villages have no clean drinking water. In such places, a borehole would bring much joy to the hearts of many. And such acts of love and mercy do open up otherwise hostile communities to the preaching of the gospel. The greatest gift that can be given to any community is education. There are communities of five thousand people or more that do not have schools. The greatest weapon against progress in life is *ignorance*. There are many nations with high percentages of widows and orphans as a result of wars in their nations. Such victims of war would listen to the message of Christ if their physical needs of food, clothing and shelter can be met.

Genesis 45:5 shows us that Joseph in Egypt became very wealthy for the purpose of preserving God's covenant people in the time of famine: *"But now, do not therefore be grieved or angry with yourselves because you sold me here; for God sent me before you to preserve life."*

How beautiful it would be to have more individuals in the Body of Christ (especially in the Church in Africa and other Third World Nations) believe and apply Deuteronomy 8:18 to their individual lives. Many have erroneously settled for poverty, thinking they are pleasing God by not having enough to support the gospel financially and materially.

Many preachers of the gospel have, over time, limited their vision to the financial abilities of the congregations they lead. Such preachers are totally controlled by the fear of the people when it comes to financial matters in their churches. Many have exited this earth completely discouraged without fulfilling their vision. And some congregations have succeeded in intimidating and controlling their ministers in money matters.

We go through the work of the gospel with such demoralizing frustrations for lack of wisdom and the knowledge of the Word of God. *Ignorance is deadly! Seek knowledge!*

THE MINISTRY OF JESUS AND THE WEALTHY

> *"Now it came to pass, afterward, that He went through every city and village, preaching and bringing the glad tidings of the kingdom of God. And the twelve were with Him, and certain women who had been healed of evil spirits and infirmities – Mary called Magdalene, out of whom had come seven demons, and Joanna the wife of Chuza, Herod's steward, and Susanne, and many others who **provided for Him from their substance**."*
> Luke 8:1-3

Jesus' followers included some members of the royal staff of His time. Though Divine, He had human sponsors. This means He gave man opportunity to participate in partnership with Him. This is God's will in the Kingdom work: that we be in partnership with Him. Our greatest challenge is the *wisdom* to teach on covenant partnerships in the gospel of our Lord Jesus Christ.

> *"Now it happened as they went that He entered a certain village; and a certain woman named Martha welcomed Him into her house. And she had a sister called Mary, who also sat at Jesus' feet and heard His word."* Luke 10:38-39

The Lord obviously stopped by often in this home to be ministered to materially. You may wish the Lord were physically present today so you can minister unto Him out of your substance. Your minister represents the Lord in your life today.

> *"Now when evening had come, because it was Preparation Day, that is, the day before the Sabbath, Joseph of Arimathea, a prominent council member, who was himself waiting for the Kingdom of God, coming and taking courage, went in to Pilate and asked for the body of Jesus. Then he* [Joseph of Arimathea] *bought fine linen, took Him down, and wrapped Him in the linen. And he laid Him in a tomb, which had been hewn out of the rock, and rolled a stone against the door of the tomb."* Mark 15:42, 43, 46

At death, Jesus was buried in a rich man's tomb – Joseph of Arimathea's personal tomb. Isaiah 53:9 says, *"And he made his grave with the wicked, and with the rich in his death ..."* God had someone prepared to give the Master a decent and befitting burial. Will a poor man have money to hew a personal tomb for himself? Many religious people would see it as a waste while souls are perishing, but God needed it. Yes, Joseph built the tomb for himself but found out he never had to use it personally at last! This is true ability to create wealth!

Many testimonies abound of believers who bought ships for their businesses and later discovered the Lord had need of such. They released them to their ministers and the ships became blessings to the kingdom of God in moving some Israelis back to their homeland. I once bought a car, which I admired and loved, for my use only to discover that I was never going to ride in it as the Lord asked me to release it to a dear missionary friend. I felt honored that I could give out a new car to another ministry in the name of the Lord.

In each of the above case, we can see God's ultimate purpose in wealth creation.

WEALTH IN THE HANDS OF THE PRESENT-DAY BELIEVER

"Most assuredly, I say to you, he who believes in Me, the works that I do he will do also; and greater works than these he will do, because I go to My Father." John 14:12

Jesus says that His believers would do greater works than He did while He was bodily present here on earth. God's intention is that we may cover the earth with the gospel of His Son. And from experience we know that this does not come easy. It takes money to preach the gospel of God's Kingdom. How on earth could exceptional ministers like Pastors Yonggi Cho of South Korea, Benny Hinn of the United States of America and E. A. Adeboye of Nigeria have achieved the great feats they accomplished, without money and wealth? Each of these men minister to millions of people in a single service. Millions come to know the Lord in a single service.

Imagine the millions that come to the Lord through the vehicle of the *media* - radio, television, print media, the Internet, etc! It costs a lot of money to accomplish this!

People do not have to go to the un-reached peoples of the earth today with limited resources. There should be a Church for every tribe, tongue and people of the earth. Missionaries should have enough resources to do the work. If you cannot leave your business to go on missions, make a covenant with the ones who have given themselves to go, by sponsoring mission projects or the missionaries themselves.

There should be massive church buildings, housing as many people as are willing to be in church every time the church doors are opened!

More Christian schools should be built and made affordable for all. There has never been such a need for Christian schools as in our time when our children are daily exposed to the dangers of drugs, illicit sex education, pornography, homosexuality, and so on.

Wealth in your hands as a believer in Christ Jesus will do great damage to the kingdom of darkness and hasten the return of our Lord to earth.

CHAPTER FIVE

A COVENANT WITH GOD—THE BASIS FOR WEALTH CREATION

The knowledge of the fact that wealth comes from God changes one's attitude towards it. Such knowledge will manifest a wholesome attitude towards wealth. As long as people believe that wealth comes from the devil they will pursue it with improper attitudes, like cheating, lying, hording, creating wealth for human destruction, etc.

A proper attitude towards wealth begins with you knowing that you are in covenant with Christ Jesus and knowing God's *purpose* in wealth creation. The Bible makes it clear that we are *covenant people with God Almighty* so you must view wealth creation as being in covenant with God. A Covenant can be described from the biblical perspective as, "A Pronouncement of God by which He establishes a relationship of Responsibility." A Covenant could be:

a. between God and an individual (e.g. Adam in the Eden Covenant, Gen. 2:16), or

b. between God and mankind in general (e.g. Noah and the flood – never again to destroy all flesh with a flood, Gen. 9:9) or

c. between God and a nation (Israel in the Mosaic Covenant,

Ex. 19:3.), or
d. between God and a specific human family (e.g. the house of David in the promise of a kingly line in perpetuity through the Davidic covenant. By this kind of covenant a promise of ultimate blessing, not only to David but also to the world in the reign of Jesus Christ, was established).

The covenants are normally unconditional in the sense that when God declares, "I will," He automatically obligates Himself in grace, to accomplish certain announced purposes, despite the failure on the part of the person or people with whom He covenants.

When Adam broke his covenant with God, God obligated Himself to accomplish His purposes with mankind despite the failure on the part of man.

When Abraham missed God and produced Ishmael, God again obligated Himself to fulfill His covenant promise to Abraham in spite of Sarah's failed scheme.

David kept his covenant with God thereby securing the promised "Throne" for his linage, but his son Solomon whose started his reign with the fear of God rounded up his reign with idol worship broke the existing covenant: God even in this case obligated Himself to accomplish His divine purpose. Jesus still came through the linage of David which is the ultimate in God's covenant with David.

> *"For the mountains may depart and the hills disappear, but even then I will remain loyal to you. My covenant of blessing will never be broken"* says the Lord, who has mercy on you.* Isaiah 54:10 (New Living Translation)

Abraham was one of the wealthiest men of his time and his covenant walk with God is evident all through his lifetime. In Genesis 12:1-3; *"Now the Lord had said to Abram: Get out of your country, from your family and from your father's house, To a land that I will show you. I will make you a great nation; I will bless you And make your name great; And you shall be a blessing. I will bless*

those who bless you, And I will curse him who curses you; And in
you all the families of the earth shall be blessed."

When God called Abraham to leave his father's house and his
kindred and go to the land of Canaan, He gave Abraham 4 personal
covenant blessings, which we can appropriate today by faith in
Christ Jesus. According to Galatians 3:13-14, *"Christ has redeemed*
us from the curse of the law, having become a curse for us (for it is
written, 'Cursed is everyone who hangs on a tree'), That the bless-
ing of Abraham might come upon the Gentiles in Christ Jesus, that
we might receive the promise of the Spirit through faith."

God's Covenant blessing to Abraham in Genesis 12: 2 are four
dimensional:

1. **THE COVENANT OF PERSONAL INCREASE** - "*... make you*
   a great nation ..." (Gen. 17:16). God was not only going to give
   him a son as Abraham understood, but he was going to make
   him—one man —into a great nation. God at the very beginning of
   creation set in motion in every creature He created, the potential to
   multiply and reproduce its kind, including man. He is the God of
   increase. God thinks BIG. He thinks in terms of generations.
   While Abraham was seeing the promise of a son, God was seeing
   in him a nation. It has never been His idea to put limitations on
   man or His other creation. So why put yourself in a box? God's
   covenant of personal increase would take more than a lifetime to
   fulfill. God did not only give Isaac to Abraham, He gave him the
   nation of Israel. The covenant of Increase also brings out the fact
   that God wants to perpetuate His blessings in our lives. God is a
   generational thinker and we must also think like Him!

   It is God's intention to give you more than you have and own
   today – land, house, car, etc. Someone somewhere in the world
   has need of the extras in your life.

2. **THE COVENANT OF PERSONAL BLESSING** - "*I will bless*
   you." This blessing is twofold: (a) spiritual and (b) temporal:

   (a). Spiritual Blessing. Gen. 15:6 says, *"And he believed in the*

Lord, and He accounted it to him for righteousness." Abraham was a man of great faith in God. The foundation of his great wealth was imbedded in his faith in God. He was a true worshipper of God. This is the primary proper attitude towards wealth that every believer in Christ should have. Your wealth creation must be rooted in your worship of God. Our new birth experience in Christ Jesus repositions us to occupy God's original intent in creating man – RULERSHIP. Salvation brings into our lives all the spiritual blessings God has for us. God intends for you to rule in dominion in the realm of the spirit as well as in the physical. The realm of the spirit can be scary as we witness intense warfare coming from there against our lives and the works of our hands. In battles, we enforce our spiritual blessings through the victory of Jesus on the cross.

Born into an idolatrous family background, I experienced first hand demonic opposition early in life. Demonic Principalities have appeared to me at each turning point in my life with great opposition to the will of God in my life. Such battles have made me a true worshipper of the living God. The intensity of those battles was usually a matter of life and death, and in such situations I had no choice but to turn to God's Word and to His worship. I fought battles at every level of advancement in life and in ministry. I fought intense battles for the lives of my two children. Battles were fought for financial breakthroughs. But in all of the battles, I testify to the glory of our great God that He gave me absolute victory!

> *"Many are the afflictions of the righteous, but the Lord delivers him out of them all."* Psalm 34:19

Worshipping God in spirit and in truth is the foundation of wealth in any believer's life. Your desire to create wealth must be rooted in your love for God: which should bring you into covenant agreement that as God blesses you, you will in turn invest it into His work for the deliverance of humanity.

(b) Temporal or physical blessing. Genesis 13:14, 15,17 says, *"And the Lord said to Abram, after Lot had separated from him: "Lift up your eyes now and look from the place where you* *are—-northward, southward, eastward, and westward; for all the land which you see I give to you and your descendants forever... Arise, walk in the land through its length and its width, for I give it to you."* - the promise of land.

Genesis 15:18 says, *"On the same day the Lord made a covenant with Abram, saying: "To your descendants I have given this land, from the river of Egypt to the great river, the River Euphrates - "*

Genesis 24:34-35 says, *"So he said, 'I am Abraham's servant. The Lord has blessed my master greatly, and he has become great; and He has given him flocks and herds, silver and gold, male and female servants, and camels and donkeys'."*

It is God's will that you rule over the "land and the things that creep on it" as well as over things beneath the soil (the mineral resources). God embedded these blessings underneath the soil for man's discovery and benefit.

It is important you believe that the Lord has a promise of parcel(s) of land for you. If you are a pastor or a minister of the gospel, this is part of your covenant with God. I shall share more on this as we progress in this study.

In Africa, land issues have taken uncountable number of lives. Most people see land matters as "unthinkable," but from the above scriptures we can see it is God's will for His people to rule in dominion over the land. Notice that wherever we desire to possess, whether the land of Canaan or any other part of the world, battles are fought first before taking possession. You must not lose heart. It is very important to God that we fight lawfully.

The Patriarchs in the Bible fought to possess the land of their promise. Sometimes they lost battles due to sin in the camp. God's temporary or physical blessings include the blessings of land and also that within the soil – mineral resources. It also includes the blessings of the heavens and those that come through the Sea. Do not let the devil cheat you out of your Covenant blessings with God. The Church has walked in poverty not because God withholds from

His own but because the Church has walked in *IGNORANCE* — what a fertile ground for demonic activities!

3. THE COVENANT OF PERSONAL HONOR - *"... And make your name great"* (Gen. 12:2)

> *"Both riches and honor come from You, and You reign over all. In Your hand is power and might; in Your hand it is to make great and to give strength to all."* 1 Chronicles 29:11-12 *(NKJV)*.

You have a covenant of *honor* with God.

> *"The Lord honors those who honor Him."* 1 Samuel 2:30

> *"The wise inherit wealth."* Proverbs 3:35

How do we define honor? I believe honor must be defined from God's perspective. *Humility* of heart and *obedience* to God's word will surely attract honor from Him.

- God brought Daniel into honor even in the land of captivity.
- Nehemiah also was in honor in the land of captivity.
- Queen Esther was likewise brought into honor for divine purpose.

In each of the three cases mentioned above, God had specific purposes for bringing them into a place of honor. Too often, for lack of understanding of God's Word, Christians seek honor from fellow men. HONOR is part of God's covenant package for you. The key to God's honor is HUMILITY of heart. Honor the Lord with your life and He will honor you with His exaltation. Abraham honored the Lord with his life, walking in covenant with God and that brought him into honor with God and men. When he arrived in the land of the Philistines, "his fear" fell on them as God rose to Abraham's defense in Genesis 20. Do not seek honor for yourself and you must discern God's purpose in bringing you into honor. Again it must be all about HIM!

4. *THE COVENANT OF BEING A CHANNEL OF BLESSING*
– *"And you will be a blessing"* (Gen. 12:2)

God's ultimate purpose in blessing anyone is that the individual will pass it on. It is in *GIVING AWAY* that God's blessings on our lives increase. *Acts 20:35 says, "… It is more blessed to give than to receive."* and 2 Corinthians 9:7 tells us that *"… God loves a cheerful giver."* Without a giving heart there is no joy in being blessed.

I believe that the United States of America has been so blessed in spite of Hollywood because they have been such channel of blessings to the entire world, especially to the Body of Christ. Think of what would have become of Africa and the so-called 'Third World Nations" if the Church in America and Europe were so stingy with their material and financial blessings. They sent Christian literature and other materials, which were of tremendous blessings to millions ever before the faces of the authors were seen through their videotapes and television programs. I came across the books of Dr. Kenneth E. Hagin in the early 1970s in Nigeria. He taught me Faith through his products. The books of Derek Prince also taught me great lessons in the ministry of Deliverance. The books of Dr. Mike Murdock taught me great Wisdom.

Some Americans and European Christians made great sacrifices by leaving their comfort zones and paid their way to different parts of the world to be a blessing. The Church in America still graciously sends help to the rest of the world in one way or another.

Africa and other Third World Countries: it is time you see your Covenant with God as a Channel of Blessing! These countries shall be more blessed when they begin to give to other nations of the world. I thank the Lord that my great nation, Nigeria has been a blessing to other African nations and beyond. Many Nigerians, who traveled to various parts of the world in search of "greener pastures" during the years of military dictatorship in Nigeria, have ended up in the ministry as missionary Pastors today. Many went overseas to further their education and ended up planting churches in the nations where they went for studies. Many Church organizations in Nigeria have planted churches in other African Countries and the world at large.

We know that God's Covenant blessings with Abraham in Genesis 12: 2 are also ours in Christ Jesus because Galatians 3:14 tells us *"that the blessing of Abraham might come upon the Gentiles in Christ Jesus, that we might receive the promise of the Spirit through faith."*

Two powerful motivators that should challenged anyone to desire to be a blessing are IGNORANCE and LACK. My heart's cry is to be a channel of blessing to Africa and other hurting nations of the world.

We know from Deuteronomy 8:18 that wealth creation is a covenant with God for the fulfillment of His Kingdom purposes. With this in mind, creating wealth will be a delight, knowing that you are working in collaboration with God as a Covenant Partner. He will bless and multiply you as long as you are willing to invest back into His Kingdom purposes. *WEALTH CREATION WITHOUT THE KNOWLEDGE OF GOD'S PURPOSE FOR IT IS DISASTROUS!*

Covenants are Renewed and Ratified by our Offerings.

After these things the word of the LORD came to Abram in a vision, saying, "Do not be afraid, Abram. I am your shield, your exceedingly great reward." But Abram said, "LORD GOD, what will You give me, seeing I go childless, and the heir of my house is Eliezer of Damascus?" Then Abram said, "Look, You have given me no offspring; indeed one born in my house is my heir!" And behold, the word of the LORD came to him, saying, "This one shall not be your heir, but one who will come from your own body shall be your heir." Then He brought him outside and said, "Look now toward heaven, and count the stars if you are able to number them." And He said to him, "So shall your descendants be." And he believed in

the LORD, and He accounted it to him for righteous-
ness. Then He said to him, "I am the LORD, who
brought you out of Ur of the Chaldeans, to give you
this land to inherit it." And he said, "Lord GOD,
how shall I know that I will inherit it?" So He said to
him, "Bring Me a three-year-old heifer, a three-year-
old female goat, a three-year-old ram, a turtledove,
and a young pigeon." Then he brought all these to
Him and cut them in two, down the middle, and
placed each piece opposite the other; but he did not
cut the birds in two. And when the vultures came
down on the carcasses, Abram drove them away.
Now when the sun was going down, a deep sleep fell
upon Abram; and behold horror and great darkness
fell upon him. Then He said to Abram: "Know
certainly that your descendants will be strangers in a
land that is not theirs, and will serve them, and they
will afflict them four hundred years. And also the
nation whom they serve I will judge; afterward they
shall come out with great possessions. Now as for
you, you shall go to your fathers in peace; you shall
be buried at a good old age. But in the fourth genera-
tion they shall return here, for the iniquity of the
Amorites is not yet complete." And it came to pass,
when the sun went down and it was dark, that behold,
there appeared a smoking oven and a burning torch
that passed between those pieces. On the same day
the LORD made a covenant with Abram, saying: "To
your descendants I have given this land, from the
river of Egypt to the great river, the River Euphrates
– the Kenites, the Kenezzites, the Kadmonites, the
Hittites, the Perizzites, the Rephaim, the Amorites,
the Canaanites, the Girgashites, and the Jebusites."
Genesis 15:1-21

God made a covenant with Abraham when He instructed him
to relocate to the land of Canaan, and promised to give it to him

and his descendants as their inheritance (Genesis 12:1-3). Fourteen years later in Genesis 15, God reiterates the same promise to Abraham strengthening the earlier promise. Abraham, at this point in his life, was going through the trail of his faith, as God's promise to give him descendants became a thing of concern, seeing he was yet to have even a son. So Abraham voiced out his concern to the Lord. God in response to Abraham's concerns about his childlessness reiterated His promise and also instructed Abraham to bring Him an offering for the ratification and renewal of His covenant with him. His offering was for the ratification of his covenant with God.

The amazing thing here is that when Abraham obeyed and offered the offerings to Him, God spoke to him prophetically on events coming up in the lives of his descendants yet unborn to the fourth generation. This is awesome! Is this not what people seek from the mystics and fortunetellers? They want to know the future, and who can tell the future as God? This particular offering from Abraham unlocked his future in God! Abraham got more than he bargained for. Yes, renew your covenants with God with your offerings!

> *"All the fighting men had taken some of the plunder for themselves. So Moses and Eleazar the priest accepted the gifts from the military commanders and brought the gold to the Tabernacle **as a reminder to the LORD that the people of Israel belong to him.**"*
> Numbers 31:54 (New Living Translation)

wisdom to multiply it. Remember the widow in 2 Kings 4:1-7; after the increase of her oil, Elisha instructed her to go and sell the oil to take care of her debts and live on the surplus.

Your offerings strengthen your covenant relationship with God.

Our discussion in the fifth chapter of this book is on our Covenant Relationship with the Lord through His sacrificial death on the cross. From the accounts of the worship of God in the Old Testament, it was obvious from the Garden of Eden when God slaughtered the first animal for the atonement of the sin of Adam and Eve to the death of Jesus Christ on the cross of Calvary, that man's relationship with God is based on covenants. Every Israelite knew that he could not approach God without a prescribed sacrifice, and this covenant relationship is sustained through more sacrifices. In the Old Testament there were much of animal sacrifices to cover the sins of God's people pending when the one and final sacrifice of Jesus Christ on the cross would be offered. Romans 10:4 says, *"For Christ is the end of the law for righteousness to everyone who believes."*

Their sacrifices were not only to cover their sins but also to strengthen and sustain their relationship with God.

Your offerings create your future

The death and resurrection of Jesus Christ brought us salvation, which includes the forgiveness of our sins. This opens us up to all the blessings of God in Christ Jesus. The blood of Jesus brings us into eternal covenant with God. Just as the people of God in the Old Testament strengthened their covenant relationship with God through the regular offerings they brought to the temple, we also should strengthen our covenant relationship with the Lord through our offerings to Him. Our financial and material offerings in the Church should not be seen as mere gifts to the Church Leaders or for the payments of bills. That places your focus on man – the Pastor or Church Leaders.

My attitude changed in the way I give my offerings the moment I learnt from God's word that my offerings in Church unlock my future. *When my offering leaves my hands it moves into my future to create my desired harvest.* I give to strengthen my covenant relationship with God based on specific scriptures related to any area of my need. God responds favorably to our offerings when offered according to His dictates.

> *"The Lord said to Moses, "Give these instructions to the people of Israel: The offerings you present to me by fire on the altar are my food, and they are very pleasing to me. See to it that they are brought at the appointed times and offered according to my instructions."* Numbers 28:1-2 (New Living Translation).

Types of Offerings in the Bible

Burnt Offerings
This is to make atonement for sin. (Leviticus 9:2; Exodus 29:15-18).

Drink Offerings
These are libations of wine offered along with other sacrifices unto God. (Genesis 35:14; Numbers 6:17).

Free Will Offering
This offering must be perfect and to be eaten by the Priests. (Leviticus 22:17-25; 7:11-18).

Heave Offering
This offering is given to the Priests' family as part of their emoluments. (Leviticus 10:14; Numbers 5:9; 18:10-19,24).

There are other kinds of offerings in the Bible such as Peace Offerings, Fellowship Offerings, and Thanksgiving Offerings.

> *"You must present these offerings to the Lord at your annual festivals. These are in addition to the sacrifices and offerings you present in connection with vows, or as freewill offerings, burnt offerings, grain offerings, drink offerings, or peace offerings."*

Numbers 29:*39* (New Living Translation)

There are several scriptural pillars of wealth creation and we shall look at five of them: *tithes, offerings, vows, almsgiving and prophets offerings.*

Tithes

> *"Will a man rob God? Yet you have robbed me! But you say, "In what way have we robbed You?" In tithes and offerings. You are cursed with a curse, for you have robbed Me, Even the whole nation. Bring all the tithes into the storehouse, That there may be food in my house, And try Me now in this," says the LORD of host, "If I will not open for you the windows of heaven And pour out for you such blessing That there will not be room enough to receive it. "And I will rebuke the devourer for your sakes, So that he will not destroy the fruit of your ground, Nor shall the vine fail to bear fruit for you in the field," says the LORD of hosts; "And all nations will call you blessed, For you will be a delightsome land, says the LORD of hosts."* Malachi 3:8-12

> *"And all the tithes of the land, whether of the seed of the land or of the fruit of the tree, is the LORD's. **It is holy to the Lord**."* Leviticus 27:30

Whenever you receive an income a tenth (10%) of it belongs to God, it is *HOLY.* Tithing is God's way of making us recognize Him as our Source. Your tithe sanctifies the rest of your income as you release it to the Lord, but when withheld it turns the rest of your income into a curse. It might interest you to know that the number "10" signifies *increase. This is God's way of increasing you.* Your tithe circumcises your financial and material life according to Malachi 3:11. Verse 12 shows us that it also beautifies your life as it brings you to a place of honor.

"Behold, I have given the children of Levi all the tithes in Israel as an inheritance in return for the work which they perform, the work of the tabernacle of meeting. Hereafter the children of Israel shall not come near the tabernacle of meeting, lest they bear sin and die. But the Levites shall perform the work of the tabernacle of meeting, and they shall bear their iniquity; it shall be a statute forever, throughout your generations, that among the children of Israel they shall have no inheritance. For the tithes of the children of Israel, which they offer up as a heave offering to the Lord, I have given to the Levites as an inheritance; therefore I have said to them, 'Among the children of Israel they shall have no inheritance.'"
Leviticus 18:21-24

The Lord is a benevolent Employer! He instituted the tithe in order to provide a means of paying His ministers here on earth, before rewarding them later in heaven. No wonder, God takes our lack of tithing very personal, He calls it robbing Him! If an employer is viewed as irresponsible for not paying his employees, how would we view God if He will not provide for the ones He has called and commissioned to work for Him on earth? It beats my imagination why the Lord will leave such an important aspect of a minister's life in the hands of the Led. I believe it is a two edged sword.

Firstly it shows the Lord's intention for the minister to depend primarily on Him as his Source. Man is by nature selfish and unwilling to share of his resources with another; therefore it takes the Lord touching the hearts of people to recognize Him as their Source, and willingly relinquish whatever is in their hands to God. This is a test of the giver's obedience and love for God.

Secondly, I believe God is teaching us the need for partnership in the kingdom work - interdependency on one another. One of the ways through which we can partner together in God's work is by fulfilling Paul's admonition in Ephesians 4:11-12, *"And He Himself gave some to be apostles, some prophets, some evangelists, and some pastors and teachers, For the equipping of the saints for the work of the ministry, for the edifying of the body of Christ, Till we all come to the unity of the faith and of the knowledge of the Son of God, to a perfect man, to the measure of the stature of the fullness of Christ;"*

I call this a division of labor in the Body of Christ. As the five-fold ministry gifts equip the saints, the saints in turn should minister back to them. Figuratively, the Christian businessperson should be seen as the queen or king who should bring in the gold for the building of God's temple from the marketplace. You must discern your area of calling as well as where God has planted you to flourish in His work (a ministry or church). Partner with your pastor/minister in the work of the ministry.

Once, I had on my staff a young man who struggled so long with his calling simply because he felt that as a university graduate, quitting his job for the ministry would jeopardize his ability to provide for his family. While I thought about this brother's concerns, the Lord spoke this parable to me in my heart. He pointed my attention to one of the wealthiest men in Nigeria at the time, Moshood Abiola. He was a known politician. He once won a Presidential Election but the military dictators denied him the opportunity to rule. The Lord said to me that if Abiola invited anyone to work for him, the individual, out of joy and excitement, would have accepted his invitation without bothering to ask him for the remuneration package, because he was a wealthy man. The invitee would have confidence in Abiola because he had enough money to pay him his wages. The individual concerned will deem it prestigious to work for such a wealthy man.

The Lord also used this other illustration about ambassadors. He said to me, "No nation sends out an ambassador to another nation without first making adequate provisions for him." The Lord then drew this conclusion for me: "Why will my children not believe in my ability to provide for them in the work of the ministry? If the world can make adequate provision for its own, why can't the Government of Heaven do much more?" Having been in the ministry of our Lord Jesus Christ for the past over 31 years of my life, I know first hand the challenges Pastors and other ministers of the gospel face in the area of raising funds for the work. The fear of the people paralyses the minister from boldly and knowledgeably raising funds for the work. I have come to the conclusion that what we all need is the scriptural knowledge of God's mind about money in His work and also, wisdom as to how to raise the money and other material resources. He has already made the provision.

This is the time the Christian in the marketplace should partner with his/her Pastor/Minister in the work of the ministry. Bring in your wealth for the television and radio ministries, for the construction of Church buildings, for mission works to the un-reached of the world.

> *"And what do I see flying like clouds to Israel, like doves to their nests? They are the ships of Tarshish, reserved to bring the people of Israel home. They will bring their wealth with them, and it will bring great honor to the Lord your God, the Holy One of Israel, for he will fill you with splendor."* Isaiah 60:8-9

Our discussions so far on tithing have been based on the individual Christian and his tithes. But the picture in Malachi 3 is that of a tithing nation. God was speaking to Israel as a nation.

The United States of America is a beautiful example of a nation that tithes. I see this in the faith based projects that their government engages in with the Church body, such as feeding the hungry and other policies that take care of the needy in their society. To me this is lending to God according to Psalm 41:1-3, *"Blessed is he who considers the poor; the Lord will deliver him in the time of trouble. The Lord will preserve him and keep him alive, and he will be blessed on the earth; You will not deliver him to the will of his enemies. The Lord will strengthen him on his bed of illness; You will sustain him on his sickbed."*

The above Bible passage makes it abundantly clear why America is so blessed by God. Wherever there is trouble on the face of the earth, especially ecological problems, floods and their likes, Americans and their government are among the first to arrive at the scene of the disaster to lend a helping hand.

I want to also liken this to a Church ministry that is blessed with a large percentage of obedient tithers. They receive the blessings of Malachi 3 as a corporate body. Such a ministry would have a number of millionaires and multi-millionaires among them. Mention must be made that the obedience to tithing for such ministry must have started from the Pastor, down to the rest of the leadership of that church. Such a ministry becomes the envy of other Pastors, *"a delightsome land."* Such a ministry allows the Lord to display His glory (His Weight) among them.

Tithes of the Priests (Number 18:25- 29): *"The LORD spoke to Moses, saying, "Speak thus to the Levites, and say to them: 'When you take from the children of Israel the tithes which I have given you from them as your inheritance, then you shall offer up a heave offering of it to the LORD, a tenth of the tithe. And your heave offering shall be reckoned to you as though it were the grain of the threshing floor and as the fullness of the winepress. Thus you shall also offer a heave offering to the LORD from all the tithes which you shall receive from the children of Israel, and you shall give the LORD's heave offering from it to Aaron the priest. Of all your gifts you shall offer up every heave offering due to the LORD, from all the best of them, the consecrated part of them."*

The Lord expects the ministers to also pay their personal tithes to Him. Seek the Lord on who you can relate with as your Pastor/Mentor – a higher anointing, especially if you are a Founding Pastor/Minister over your work and pay your personal tithe to him or her.

B. Offerings

> *"And if you offer a sacrifice of a peace offering to the Lord, you shall offer it of your own free will."*
> Leviticus. 19:5

A study of Israel's worship of God in the Old Testament reveals that whenever anyone went to the temple, he went with his offerings for specific areas of need. Even after a healing, one is expected to offer a sacrifice to the Lord. Jesus, after declaring the man He healed of leprosy whole, told him to take an offering to the temple as part of his testimonial as he presented himself to the priest. God says that no man should appear before Him empty-handed. God's people must be taught that He expects us to come into His presence with our money-seeds as our sacrifices to Him. Our worship is not complete without our offerings.

*"You shall keep the Feast of Unleavened Bread (you shall eat unleavened bread seven days, as I commanded you, at the appointed time in the month of Abib, for in it you came out of Egypt; **none shall appear before Me empty);"** Exodus 23:15*

*"But the first born of a donkey you shall redeem with a lamb. And if you will not redeem him, then you shall break his neck. All the first born of your sons you shall redeem. **And none shall appear before Me empty**." Exodus. 34:20*

*"Three times a year all your males shall appear before the LORD your God in the place which He chooses: at the feast of Unleavened Bread, at the Feast of Weeks, and at the feast of Tabernacles; and **they shall not appear before the Lord empty-handed**." Deuteronomy.16:16*

"Whatever has a defect, you shall not offer, for it shall not be acceptable on your behalf." Leviticus. 22:20

This verse of the Bible teaches the importance of bringing to God, clean and healthy offerings. In environments where people do not respect their country's currency, people bring to church as their offerings, torn and dirty currency notes. This should not be so. God does not allow it.

Pre-plan Your Offerings

"Now concerning the ministering to the saints, it is superfluous for me to write to you; for I know your

willingness, about which I boast of you to the Macedonians, that Achaia was ready a year ago; and your zeal has stirred up the majority. Yet I have sent the brethren, lest our boasting of you should be in vain in this respect, that as I said, you may be ready; lest if some Macedonians come with me and find you unprepared, we (not to mention you!) should be ashamed of this confident boasting. Therefore I thought it necessary to exhort the brethren to go to you ahead of time, and prepare your generous gift beforehand, which you had previously promised, that it may be ready as a matter of generosity and not as a grudging obligation." 2 Corinthians 9:1-5

Offerings are one of the ways covenants are ratified before God. Many Christians do not have the understanding of their offering being a means of both cutting and strengthening their covenant relationship with God. Many offer their offerings to God as a grudging obligation; some even come before the Lord EMPTY HANDED! When it is offering time in church, some believers search their wallets for whatever amount of money they can find to give at the spur of the moment.

Always ask the Holy Spirit for the amount of offering to give in any given service. God prescribed the Old Testament offerings. People did not just give any amount of offering they felt like giving. There were specific instructions on what to bring and the quantity to bring as offerings to the Lord. In some services the preacher may call out a certain amount of money or some specific offerings. All of this is scriptural.

Giving Willingly and Joyfully!

"But this I say; He who sows sparingly will also reap sparingly, and he who sows bountifully will also reap bountifully. So let each one give as he purposes in his heart, not grudgingly or of necessity; **For God loves a cheerful giver**.*"* 2 Corinthians 9:6-7

There are two reasons why I give: firstly, because of the Lord Himself (He is the Rewarder of His worshippers) and secondly, my desired harvest (It can never fail!). When the Lord is the object of our giving, we shall give joyfully and bountifully. I always look forward to the offering time as an investment time with God. I bring my offerings to Him with my eyes set on the harvest rather than on my lack. My joy as I release my offerings to the Lord is in His ability to give me a harvest.

> *"While the earth remains, seedtime and harvest, cold and heat, winter and summer, day and night shall not cease"* Genesis 8:22

> *"Moreover, brethren, we make known to you the grace of God bestowed on the churches of Macedonia: That in a great trail of affliction the abundance of their **joy** and their deep poverty abounded in the riches of their liberality. For I bear witness that according to their ability, yes, and beyond their ability, they were **freely willing**, Imploring us with much urgency that we would receive the gift and the fellowship of the ministering to the saints."* 2 Corinthians 8:1-4

C. Vows

Vows were voluntary promises which, when made, were to be kept if the thing vowed was right. They were made under a great variety of circumstances. Vows attract the favor and mercies of God. Its nature is two-fold, you promise the Lord a gift (animate or inanimate) when He fulfils it, you pay your vow.

> *"Now Jacob went out from Beersheba and went toward Haran. So he came to a certain place and stayed there all night, because the sun has set. And he took one of the stones of that place and put it at his head, and he lay down in that place to sleep.*

Then he dreamed, and behold, a ladder was set up on the earth, and its top reached to heaven: and there the angels of God were ascending and descending on it. And behold, the LORD stood above it and said; "I am the LORD God of Abraham your father and the God of Isaac: the land on which you lie I will give to you and your descendants. Also your descendants shall be as the dust of the earth; you shall spread abroad to the west and the east, to the north and the south; and in you and in your seed all the families of the earth shall be blessed. Behold, I am with you and will keep you wherever you go, and will bring you back to this land: for I will not leave you until I have done what I have spoken to you." Then Jacob awoke from his sleep and said, "Surely the LORD is in this place, and I did not know it." And he was afraid and said, "How awesome is this place! This is none other than the house of God, and this is the gate of heaven!" Then Jacob rose early in the morning, and took the stone that he had put at his head, set it up as a pillar, and poured oil on top of it. And he called the name of that place Bethel: but the name of that city had been Luz previously. Then Jacob made a vow, saying, "If God will be with me, and keep me in this way that I am going, and give me bread to eat and clothing to put on, So that I come back to my father's house in peace, then the LORD shall be my God. And this stone which I have set as a pillar shall be God's house, and of all that You give me I will surely give a tenth to You." Gen. 28: 10-22

"Then Moses spoke to the heads of the tribes concerning the children of Israel, saying, 'This is the thing which the LORD has commanded: If a man makes a vow to the Lord, or swears an oath to bind himself by an agreement, he shall not break his

word; he shall do according to all that proceeds out of his mouth'." Numbers 30:1-2 (I recommend you read the entire chapter)

"You shall not bring the wages of a harlot or the price of a dog to the house of the LORD your God for any vowed offering, for both of these are an abomination to the LORD your God... When you make a vow to the LORD, you shall not delay to pay it; for the LORD your God will surely require it of you, and it will be sin to you." Deuteronomy 23:18, 21

"And Jephthah made a vow to the LORD, and said, "If You will indeed deliver the people of Ammon into my hands, then it will be that whatever comes out of the doors of my house to meet me, when I return in peace from the people of Ammon, shall surely be the LORD's, and I will offer it up as a burnt offering... And it was so at the end of two months that she returned to her father, and he carried out his vow with her which he had vowed. She knew no man. And it became a custom in Israel." Judges 11:30, 31,39

"And she was in bitterness of soul, and prayed to the LORD and wept in anguish. Then she made a vow and said, "O LORD of hosts, if You will indeed look on the affliction of your maidservant and remember me, and not forget Your maidservant, but will give Your maidservant a male child, then I will give him to the LORD all the days of his life, and no razor shall come upon his head." 1 Samuel 1: 10,11

"Also Paul still remained a good while. Then he took leave of the brethren and sailed for Syria, and Priscilla and Aquila were with him. He has his hair cut off at Cenchrea, for he had taken a vow." Acts 18:18

D. Offerings for the Poor

> *"He who has pity on the poor lends to the LORD,*
> *and He will pay back what He has given."*
> Proverbs. 19:17

Giving to the poor is lending to the Lord and the Lord can never owe anyone! Providing for the poor is based on the principle of surplus or extras. This will be discussed fully in Chapter 8.

> *"When you reap the harvest of your land, you shall*
> *not wholly reap the corners of your field, nor shall*
> *you gather the gleanings of your harvest. And you*
> *shall not glean your vineyard, nor shall you gather*
> *every grape of your vineyard; you shall leave them*
> *for the poor and the stranger: I am the LORD your*
> *God."* Leviticus 19:9,10

The Poor were given the right to glean the fields of others during the harvest seasons. This is a principle put in place by God for the provision of the Poor among His people. This was the principle that enabled Ruth in the Bible to find Boaz. God cares a lot for the Poor and we should also care. We must take note of the fact that providing for the Poor is a deliberate step towards helping them. There must be the willing mind to provide for them.

> *"When you reap your harvest in your field, and*
> *forget a sheaf in the field, you shall not go back to*
> *get it; it shall be for the stranger, the fatherless, and*
> *the widow, that the LORD your God may bless you*
> *in all the work of your hands. When you gather the*
> *grapes of your vineyard, you shall not glean it after-*
> *ward; it shall be for the stranger, the fatherless, and*
> *the widow."* Deuteronomy 24:19, 21

In the sabbatical year they were to have their share of the produce of the fields and the vineyards.

"But the seventh year you shall let it rest and lie fallow, that the poor of your people may eat; and what they leave, the beasts of the field may eat. In like manner you shall do with your vineyard and your olive grove." Exodus 23:11

The Poor recovered their property in the year of Jubilee:

"If one of your brethren becomes poor, and has sold some of his possession, and if his redeeming relative comes to redeem it, then he may redeem what his brother sold. Or if the man has no one to redeem it, but he himself becomes able to redeem it, then let him count the years since its sale, and restore the remainder to the man to whom he sold it, that he may return to his possession. But if he is not able to have it restored to himself, then what was sold shall remain in the hand of him who bought it until the Year of Jubilee; and in the Jubilee it shall be released, and he shall return to his possession." Leviticus 25:25-28

The rich were to be generous to the poor:

"If there is among you a poor man of your brethren, within any of the gates in your land which the LORD your God is giving you, you shall not harden your heart nor shut your hand from your poor brother, but you shall open your hand wide to him and willingly lend him sufficient for his need, whatever he needs. Beware lest there be a wicked thought in your heart, saying, 'The seventh year, the year of release, is at hand,' and your eye be evil against your poor brother and you give him nothing, and he cry out to the Lord against you, and it become sin against you. You shall surely give to him, and your heart should not be grieved when you give to him, because for this thing the LORD your God will bless you in all

*your works and in all to which you put your hand.
For the poor will never cease from the land; therefore I command you, saying, 'You shall open your
hand wide to your brother, to your poor and your
needy, in your land."* Deuteronomy 15:7-11

In the Sabbatical and Jubilee years the bondservant was to go free:

*"If your brother, a Hebrew man, or a Hebrew
woman, is sold to you and serves you six years, then
in the seventh year you shall let him go free from
you. And when you send him away free from you,
you shall not let him go away empty-handed; You
shall supply him liberally from your flock, from your
threshing floor, and from your winepress. From what
the LORD your God has blessed you with, you shall
give to him. You shall remember that you were a
slave in the land of Egypt, and the LORD your God
redeemed you; therefore I command you this thing
today."* Deuteronomy 15:12-15

Certain portions from the tithes were assigned to the poor:

*"At the end of every third year you shall bring out the tithe of
your produce of that year and store it up within your gates. And the
Levite, because he has no portion nor inheritance with you, and the
stranger and the fatherless and the widow who are within your
gates, may come and eat and be satisfied, that the LORD your God
may bless you in all the work of your hand which you do."*
Deuteronomy 14:28, 29

This is a form of investment for the needy and the Levite.

*"When you have finished laying aside all the tithe of
your increase in the third year-the year of tithing-and
have given it to the Levite, the stranger, the fatherless,*

and the widow, so that they may eat within your gates and be filled, then you shall say before the LORD your God: 'I have removed the holy tithe from my house, and also have given them to the Levite, the stranger, the fatherless, and the widow, according to all Your commandments which You have commanded me; I have not transgressed Your commandments, nor have I forgotten them." Deuteronomy 26:12, 13

The Poor shared in the feasts:

"You shall rejoice before the LORD your God, you and your son and your daughter, your male servant and your female servant, the Levite who is within your gates, the stranger and the fatherless and the widow who are among you, at the place where the LORD your God chooses to make His name abide. And you shall rejoice in your feast, you and your son and your daughter, your male servant and your female servant and the Levite, the stranger and the fatherless and the widow, who are within your gates." Deuteronomy 16:11, 14

Wages were to be paid at the close of each day:

"You shall not cheat your neighbor, nor rob him. The wages of him who is hired shall not remain with you all night until morning." Leviticus 19:13

Begging was not common under the Old Testament, but it was present in the New Testament times (Luke 16:20, 21 – Lazarus and the rich man). However, begging in the case of those who are able to work was forbidden, and all such were enjoined to "work with their own hands" as a Christian duty (1 Thessalonians 4:11).

For you yourselves know how you aught to follow us, for we were not disorderly among you; nor did we eat anyone's bread free of charge, but worked with labor and toil night and day, that we might not be a burden to any of you, not because we do not have authority, but to make ourselves an example of how you should follow us. For even when we were with you, we commanded you this: If anyone will not work, neither shall he eat. For we hear that there are some who walk among you in disorderly manner, not working at all, but are busybodies. Now those who are such command and exhort through our Lord Jesus Christ that they work in quietness and eat their own bread. 2 Thessalonians 3:7-13

I have taken time to list out the above passages of the Bible to help us see the Poor among us through God's eyes. We can begin to see from this point that God's purposes for wealth creation are beyond our selfish desires. In tithing God intends that His people should willingly provide for His Ministers and here, in matters pertaining to the Poor, God also wants us to be our brother's keeper. This is why you must aspire to create wealth for the purpose of *being a blessing*. We shall revisit this issue in Chapters 8.

E. Prophets Offerings

"Then the word of the LORD came to him, saying, "Arise, go to Zarephath, which belongs to Sidon, and dwell there. See, I have commanded a widow there to provide for you." So he arose and went to Zarephath. And when he came to the gate of the city, indeed a widow was there gathering sticks. And he called to her and said, "Please bring me a little water in a cup, that I may drink." And as she was going to get it, he called to her and said, "Please bring me a morsel of bread in your hand." So she said, "As the LORD your God lives, I do not have bread, only a handful of flour in a bin, and a little oil in a jar: and see, I am gathering a couple of sticks

that I may go in and prepare it for myself and my son, that we may eat it and die." And Elijah said to her, "Do not fear: go and do as you have said, but make me a small cake from it first, and bring it to me: and afterward make some for yourself and your son. For thus says the LORD God of Israel; 'The bin of flour shall not be used up nor shall the jar of oil run dry, until the day the LORD sends rain on the earth.'" So she went away and did according to the word of Elijah: and she and he and her household ate for many days. The bin of flour was not used up, nor did the jar of oil run dry, according to the word of the LORD, which He spoke by Elijah. Now it happened after these things that the son of the woman who owned the house became sick. And his sickness was so serious that there was no breath left in him. So she said to Elijah, "What have I to do with you, O man of God? Have you come to me bring my sin to remembrance, and to kill my son?" And he said to her, "Give me your son." So he took him out of her arms and carried him to the upper room where he was staying, and laid him on his own bed. Then he cried out to the LORD and said, "O LORD my God, have you also brought tragedy on the widow with whom I lodge, by killing her son?" And he stretched himself out on the child three times, and cried out to the LORD and said, "O LORD my God, I pray, let this child's soul come back to him." Then the LORD heard the voice of Elijah; and the soul of the child came back to him, and he revived. And Elijah took the child and brought him down from the upper room into the house, and gave him to his mother. And Elijah said, "See, your son lives!" Then the woman said to Elijah, "Now by this I know that you are a man of God, and that the word of the LORD in your mouth is the truth." 1 Kings 17: 8-24

The Heave offering in the Bible sounds to me like the Prophet's offering. The scenario in 1 Kings 17 reveals God's supernatural way of providing for His own. Elijah the Prophet was in need of shelter and food. Though he pronounced the judgment on the nation as a result of their idolatry, he also partook of the drought. God made an arrangement for Elijah's provision through a widow in Zarephath who was also in need of food for survival. Here is a beautiful picture of partnership. The widow's obedience to Elijah's instructions brought the needed miracle into her life. *Your miracle depends on your obedience to God's instructions and that of His Prophets.*

It must be emphasized that this means of divine provision sets up both the giver and the receiver for divine intervention. For Elijah we can deduce the following:

1. Knowing the cultural beliefs about widows (poor, destitute, social outcasts), it was definitely not easy for the Prophet to ask a widow for material help at the time of famine. But he knew to obey the Lord! Elijah was working on terms of God's Covenant relationship that cannot fail.
2. Elijah was not to pay the widow a one time visit and leave, but was to reside in her home until the Lord sent help another way at the end of the famine. He could have missed God if he was obsessed with people's opinion rather than with God's instructions. Yes, he knew to obey God. Often a one-time offering isn't enough for our divine release.
3. Elijah's pride and ego could have hindered both his miracle and that of the widow, and thereby deny the Lord God of his glory and honor. He could have chosen to do it his way and not God's way and the results would have being more fleshly than spiritual.

For the widow we can deduce the following:

1. She could have missed God by looking at the Prophet as the one placing the demand on her. *She was able to discern her prophet.* She knew Elijah as God's Man who could bring her

the Word of God. She saw beyond the Prophet and saw God behind the demand. She must have understood God's covenant.

2. She must have understood how a covenant works for parties involved in one. She gave her last meal with hope that the terms of the covenant would not fail her. And they did not fail her.

3. She gave from what she had. She did not have to give to God's Man from what she did not have. Give according to your ability. Give it right *now* do not procrastinate!

4. Her meal might have being small in size *but it was her last meal.* This sounds like the widow's mite in the New Testament. It was all she had!

5. Her harvests lasted beyond the famine as the Prophet resided in her home and her giving was made continuous.

6. When death penetrated her home and stole her son from her, her gifts that had already made room for her; gave her access to the Prophet and she received another miracle of a revived son! *Discern your prophets and start your investments!*

7. Could it be that God sent Elijah to her for her survival during the famine as well as for the future restoration of her son? God delivers us from unseen attacks. Ecclesiastes 11:1-2 tells us to: *"Cast your bread upon the waters, for you will find it after many days. Give a serving to seven, and also to eight, for you do not know what evil will be on the earth."* Your covenant seeds preserve your future.

From God's perspective we deduce the following:

1. God waits for your obedience to His instructions before He can release His plans for your miracles. His plans will unfold based on your obedience to His first instructions. Two big problems with instructions from God is that they appear so simple that they might be ignored; secondly God does not change His instructions just because we are in doubt. We can see an example in the story of Naaman and Elisha – *"Go and wash in the River Jordan seven times, and your flesh shall be*

restored to you, and you shall be clean." (2 Kings 5:10);
Mary the mother of Jesus in John 2: 5, *"Whatever He says to
you, do it"* Their obedience turned water into wine.

2. The physical appearance of God's minister may not appeal
   to you, he may not be as intelligent as expected, his methods
   may not excite you, yet his instructions must be obeyed.

3. You must be able to discern God's instructions coming to
   you through His Prophet in your life.

4. God works out your miracles for you through you! He will
   always need your cooperation! To bring about the conception
   and delivery of a baby, God needs the cooperation of both
   parents.

5. He is a covenant keeping God. He did not fail the obedient in
   the past so He will never fail us in the present or in the future!

The issue of giving is all about a covenant relationship with
God and the joy in this relationship is that we are dealing with a
Partner who can never fail – God!

> *"Now it happened one day that Elisha went to
> Shunem, where there was a notable woman, and she
> persuaded him to eat some food. So it was, as often
> as he passed by, he would turn in there to eat some
> food. And she said to her husband, "Look now, I
> know that this is a holy man of God, who passes by
> us regularly. Please, let us make a small upper room
> on the wall; and let us put a bed for him there, and a
> table and a chair and a lampstand; so it will be,
> whenever he comes to us, he can turn in there." And
> it happened one day that he came there, and he
> turned in to the upper room and lay down there. Then
> he said to Gehazi his servant, "Call this Shunammite
> woman." When he had called her, she stood before
> him. And he said to him, "Say now to her, 'Look you
> have been concerned for us with all this care. What
> can I do for you? Do you want me to speak on your
> behalf to the king or to the commander of the army?"*

She answered, "I dwell among my own people." So he said, "What then is to be done for her?" And Gehazi answered, "Actually, she has no son, and her husband is old." So he said, "Call her." When he had called her, she stood in the doorway. Then he said, "About this time next year you shall embrace a son." And she said, "No, my lord. Man of God, do not lie to your maidservant!" 2 Kings 4:8-16

Lessons from the rich woman:

1. She was not poor so she was not giving to the Prophet because of a need. She just had understanding about being in covenant with God's Prophet.
2. But Elisha the prophet, knowing that every gift to him in the name of the Lord is a covenant that has a reward, demanded that the rich woman request for a harvest. He helped her identify her harvest...a son.
3. She was able to *discern her prophet.* The ability to discern when God sends a prophet or a prophetic word your way is the key to your miracle. *Discern your Prophet.*
4. Her covenant seed brought a miracle son into her life. Your seed will always create your desired harvest.
5. When death crept in and stole her miracle (just as in the case of the widow), she adamantly placed a demand on the terms of the covenant. Know the terms of God's covenants with you; He will come through for you.
6. Her stolen miracle (her son) was restored back to her. In Matthew 7:7-11, Jesus said that we should keep knocking until the door is opened. The devil often would attack your harvest, do not let your heart fail you. Persistency will force the enemy to release his grip on your stolen miracle.

"Then Elisha spoke to the woman whose son he had restored to life, saying, 'Arise and go, you and your household, and stay wherever you can; for the LORD has called for a famine, and furthermore, it will come

upon the land for seven years.' So the woman arose and did according to the saying of the man of God, and she went with her household and dwelt in the land of the Philistine seven years. And it came to pass, at the end of seven years, that the woman returned from the land of the Philistine; and she went to make an appeal to the king for her house and for her land. Then the king talked with Gehazi the servant of the man of God, saying, "Tell me, please, all the great things Elisha has done." Now it happened, as he was telling the king how he had restored the dead to life, that there was the woman whose son he had restored to life, appealing to the king for her house and her land. And Gehazi said, "My lord, O king, this is the woman, and this is her son whom Elisha restored to life." And when the king asked the woman, she told him. So the king appointed a certain officer for her, saying, "Restore all that was hers, and all the proceeds of the field from the day that she left the land until now." 2 Kings 8:1-6

More lessons from the rich woman:

1. Her harvest exceeded her immediate need of a son, went into her future and preserved her life and that of her child. She received "a prophetic privileged information" about a divine judgment coming on the land (famine) – Word of Knowledge. God often would endear you to the heart of His prophet through your generous offerings and you will be constantly borne before the Lord in his/her prayers.
2. She was given divine direction on how to secure her future with that of her household for seven years (Word of Wisdom).
3. Seven years later she was before the king in honor. The testimony of her miracle son brought her honor before the king.
4. She recovered all she lost in the seven years of famine –a thousand times more! What a mighty God we serve! He is surely the Rewarder of them who diligently seek Him. Enter

into covenant relationship with His minister and reap an endless harvest.

The Prophet's Reward:

> *"He who receives you receives Me, and he who receives Me receives Him who sent Me. He who receives a prophet in the name of a prophet shall receive a prophet's reward."* Matthew 10:40-41

The Lord Jesus Christ in the above passage of scripture promises a prophet's reward for our obedience to His instructions through His prophets.

CHAPTER SEVEN

PRINCIPLES OF WEALTH CREATION

Principles are sets of rules or laws that guide and sustain life generally, like sets of moral laws, laws of nature...gravity... laws that sustain God's creation.... In the context of these studies principles of wealth creation as seen in the bible will serve as our guideline too not only to create wealth but also to sustain it. When principles are respected the desired effect will be the result but once violated things will fall apart. They are like pillars to any structure. The principles of wealth creation favor both the righteous and the unrighteous, depending on who obeys the rules.

1. Desire

The world has no difficulty in making up their minds about whatever they want. The believer in Christ Jesus seems to have difficulties in making up his mind as regarding his desire. I presume the reason is the love for the Lord, which keeps the believer not wanting to miss Him; as a result there is so much indecision in what should or should not be desired. God planted the ability to desire things in humans unlike the animal world. Desire gives the ability to make choices.

When the Lord responded in a night vision to the abundance of Solomon's sacrifices, He asked him what he desired from Him. (1 Kings 3:5).

In Mark 11:24; Jesus says, *"Therefore, I say unto you, whatever things ye desire, when you pray, believe that ye receive them, and ye shall have them."* (KJV).

Psalm 37:4 says, *"Delight yourself also in the LORD, and He shall give you the desire of your heart."*

It is no sin to desire to be wealthy especially if that desire is to expand the kingdom of God. And God will surely honor such desires. Without desire there will be no fuel to keep the flame of your dream burning in the face of all odds. The fuel of your desire ignites your purpose in life. Faith must lay hold on desire to attain the set goal. Arm a poor man with a strong desire to create wealth and in no time he will be seen at the top of the ladder of success.

The proof of your desire is your pursuit.

It is not good enough to desire to have wealth; you must invest quality *time and study,* investigating how the wealthy obtained their wealth. Read and study books written by such people. In cases where you have direct access to such individuals, take advantage and seek an appointment. Have your questions ready before meeting with such busy minds. You must have your journal and pen ever ready to take notes because every word from such great minds is loaded with wisdom. Their words are loaded with wisdom from many years of experience. Watch out for opportunities that might come your way. It is said that success occurs when opportunity meets with preparation.

2. Cultivate a Culture of Saving as Against a Culture of Spending

I was once sharing thoughts on principles of wealth creation with a minister friend. He asked me what I thought the Lord meant when He said 'give and it shall be given to you' in Luke 6:38. To my friend that scripture meant spending all you receive for the gospel's sake. This is the culture we all inherited – a spending culture - and the same is unconsciously passed down to our children. Read this, *"The wise have wealth and luxury, but fools spend whatever they get."* Proverbs 21:20 (New Living Translation)

Secular education prepares people to work for money. Every university graduate leaves College with high expectations of finding a "good and respectable job" that will attract a handsome income. As the new job is secured with excitement and time rolls on, the excitement may turn to frustration, as there is always an increase in the desire to improve one's status. Meeting the demands of the status quo in the society calls for more spending: a better home in an exclusive area, designer dresses and shoes to match, the list is endless. This might lead to a frequent change in jobs. With time, one discovers that working for money does not really accumulate wealth. Some may attempt to save part of their income but once there is any challenge requiring money, the savings are terminated to meet the "urgent need."

I learnt from the wealthy to save 30% of my income. The first 10% is my tithe, the next 10% is for my stockbroker and the third 10% is towards investments. The remaining 70% is for my recurrent expenditures. When I tried this principle I was pleasantly surprised that I pulled through the month, keeping my recurrent needs within the 70%. This is the first practical principle in wealth creation. The wealthy do not go after pleasurable goods immediately they earn some income. Rather, they have a habit of saving 30% first.

There are 3 lessons to learn from the wealthy here: First, you learn to live below your income. Second, you learn to seek counsel from the wealthy. Third, you learn to make your money work for you.

3. Cultivate a Culture of Budgeting

I suppose many may have a culture of budgeting, but the discipline of implementation is where the challenge lies. You must curtail your expenses. Make a difference between your real needs and your pleasurable wants. Your desires will always be more than your income; this is where the control that comes through budgeting becomes a blessing. In budgeting, you must start with the 30%

savings method mentioned above. This must not be touched. Then go on to write down a list of all your recurrent needs and cross out any unnecessary expenses. Keep adjusting the budget to increase your savings. See your pleasurable wants as paying out money to others thereby increasing them while you deflate your income. The world knows how to get us to spend our money through the frequent loud screaming adverts on the television screens. View such spending as increasing the wealth of the producers of the products while you reduce your savings. You increase their wealth while you decrease yours. You must determine your real needs before spending. This philosophy helps me evaluate my reasons for shopping.

4. *Cultivate a Culture of Profitable Investments.*

Cultivating the culture of saving part of your income is just the beginning of wealth creation. The next and most important step in wealth creation is investments. We have been taught that a person's wealth is measured by the size of his bank account. This is an illusion. The wealth of a person is not in the amount he carries around or the amount he has for spending; rather it is measured by his investments. Your investments bring you continual income whether you work or not. This is where the Parable of the Talents in Matthew 25:14-30, fits. The Lord believes in this principle of investment. The first investor in this parable traded with his talent; in other words he increased what was initially given to him, likewise the second investor. The wicked and slothful servant who did not invest his talent did not only lose it, he suffered for his foolishness. His talent was taken from him and given to the person who had become skilled in his own investment abilities. Often one hears some Christians antagonize other Christians that give regularly to the 'big ministries', instead of investing 'in the smaller and poor ministries'. The principle is seen in this parable given by the Lord Jesus Himself. No one will like to invest in redundant companies. People always look out for companies that are viable to invest their money. Likewise Christians should invest in ministries that have a great vision of soul winning and enriching the body of Christ. When you imbibe the culture of investing, it does not just increase you, it multiplies your income. As you increase your ability to invest, you can have multiple investments with multiple incomes.

5. Seek Professional Help for the Security of Your Funds.

The investor must protect his investments strictly. The first principle of protecting your investment is the security of the investment. Friends and family are always at hand to help spend our principal by asking for loans. Before releasing your hard earned money as a loan, be sure of the ability of the individual concerned to pay back, else it becomes a gift and precious relationships go sour.

Do not get involved with money mongers who promise to multiply your money in the most questionable ways, a "get rich quick" game. You are bound to lose everything.

The safest way to multiply your money is through experienced professionals. Pay the professionals to invest your money for you – the lawyers, accountants and the stockbrokers – especially as your business grows.

6. Invest in Real Estate

The lessons learnt from budgeting could accelerate the multiplication of one's income, bringing you to the next profitable investment – your home. In a culture where loans are somewhat easily obtained from financial institutions, one may take a loan and complete a home while spreading the repayments to cover the rent, usually paid to the landlord. But in cultures where it is very difficult to obtain such loans, the habit of saving cultivated over time will make the owning of a home much easier. There is nothing as fulfilling as owning your own home. It is also a way of cutting down on your expenses in certain cultures.

7. Foresight and Good Judgment

Jesus told the parable below which teaches numerous lessons on the principle of a foresight and good judgment.

*"He also said to His disciples: "There was a certain
rich man who had a steward, and an accusation was
brought to him that this man was wasting his goods.
So he called him and said to him, 'What is this I
hear about you? Give account of your stewardship,
for you can no longer be steward.' Then the steward
said within himself, 'What shall I do? For my master
is taking the stewardship away from me. I cannot
dig; I am ashamed to beg. I have resolved what to
do, that when I am put out of the stewardship, they
may receive me into their houses.' So he called every
one of his master's debtors to him, and said to the
first, 'How much do you owe my master?' And he
said, 'A hundred measures of oil.' So he said to him,
'Tale your bill, and sit down quickly and write fifty.'
Then he said to another, 'And how much do you
owe? So he said, A hundred measures of wheat.' And
he said to him, 'Take your bill, and write eighty.' So
the master commended the unjust steward because
he had dealt shrewdly. For the sons of this world are
more shrewd in their generation than the sons of
light. "And I say to you, make friends for yourselves
by unrighteous mammon, that when you fail, they
may receive you into an everlasting home. He who is
faithful in what is least is faithful also in much; and
he who is unjust in what is least is unjust also in
much. Therefore if you have not been faithful in the
unrighteous mammon, who will commit to your trust
the true riches? And if you have not been faithful in
what is another man's, who will give you what is
your own? No servant can serve two masters; for
either he will hate the one and love the other, or else
he will be loyal to the one and despise the other. You
cannot serve God and mammon."* Luke 16:1-13

Lessons Jesus taught on the Unjust Steward:

It is noteworthy that Jesus actually taught lessons on money and business management. Some religious Christians would rather spiritualize this parable than let it be what the Master intended.

1. Though the Unjust Servant was unfaithful to his master, he was **shrewd**. That means, *good at judging what people or situations are really like, especially in a way that makes you successful*. He was true to himself about his present situation and that enabled him to discern right. This is similar to the experience of Jacob while managing his uncle Laban's business. He was able to discern Laban's motives and actions, thereby making the appropriate decisions at the right time; to remove his family from further manipulations. Making the best out of every ugly situation (Luke 16: 8-9).
2. He had *foresight*. He had the ability to turn his failure into success by believing in his future. He did not call a pity party neither did he slum into depression. He was forward looking. He was a visionary leader.
3. He had the ability to manage human relations.

More lessons from the Parable:

1. Use the money-power to create healthy and lasting relationships for your future.
2. *Good management of money* qualifies you as the recipient of true riches, (spiritual gifts, as Jesus said in verse 10). Trustworthiness is a great virtue in wealth creation. It is amazing that Jesus would draw an analogy between managing money and managing spiritual riches and use it as criterion for receiving spiritual gifts. Little wonder the devil celebrates our ignorance on money matters.
3. *Faithfulness in serving others*: The ability to serve others faithfully qualifies one for one's own wealth, business, ministry, etc. Faithfulness begins with little. Joseph was at all times faithful in service, whether in taking some meals to his

elder brothers in the bush or in Potipher's home or interpreting other people's dreams in prison. David served King Saul to the point of death. None of these two lost their rewards.

4. *Who is in charge, God or Mammon (money)?* God is either the Master over your life or money is. Both cannot be Masters at the same time. *Worship the Lord and let money serve you!*

8. *Provide for the Rainy Days.*

Herein lies the greatest deception of the devil in the Church concerning wealth. Many Christians believe they will live long on earth, claiming God's covenant promises on longevity of life. But they rarely plan towards it. Each believes God would provide for them no matter what. The plan to create wealth towards their old age is non-existent. Others who invest towards their old age do not include their families in their plans; very few people make provisions for their families even after their demise. A conscious effort to invest in one's future will become a healthy attitude towards investing for Kingdom purposes.

There are safe ways to invest into your future, like buying lands and houses. Real Estate will, most of the time, appreciate in value. Investments of this nature will make your financial contributions to the gospel more substantial. I had mentioned earlier of a Christian millionaire who, through the instructions of the Holy Spirit, started a business primarily for the furtherance of God's kingdom. Does it not amaze you that the people of the world have sense enough to do all we are studying in this book yet some Christians refuse to do as much as plan for their future?

We should be like our Father in heaven who planned the salvation of man from eternity past and was patient enough to see its manifestation thousands of years later. God has been planning the marriage supper of His Son from eternity past, and it is yet to manifest. He is a long-range Planner! Friend, sit up and change your attitude towards life! It is never too late.

We must face the reality of growing old. A study in the book of Ecclesiastes 12 will show how the human body deteriorates with the wear and tear of age. Even if you claim all the faith you want, the body tells you it is no longer as strong as it used to be and needs special attention if it is to carry on a little longer. For some, growing old brings a lot of health conditions that require substantial spending and without a planned future, death will be very close by. Be wise!

9. Increase your Ability to Earn More

The ability to increase your earning capacity will mostly depend on that strong inner passion called desire. You must desire to increase and earn more. Another element to help your ability to increase and earn more is the quality of being specific in your goal setting. The mere wish to become wealthy and rich will not take one too far. That is more like a vague desire but to desire to make twice or triple your present income in specific known figures gives you an attainable goal. Once you are specific on your goals, it becomes easier to achieve, and gives a sense of attainment.

Ability to discipline one's self in goal setting and budgeting will make multiple streams of income possible.

This is the practical way to create wealth. It is not a "get rich quick" scheme.

If we teach these principles to our children, they will not only maintain their inheritance but will also teach the generations of their own children the same lessons, and the society will change for the better while the church will experience unprecedented prosperity in spreading the gospel.

Imbibing the principles studied in this section of this book will definitely put you on the part of rulership over wealth.

SECTION TWO

Wealth is of God. Jesus associated with the poor as well as the wealthy. He taught great lessons on money and drew analogies between money and spiritual things. He had some of the wealthy of His time as His partners.

Our relationship with God is based on covenant with Him. The death of Christ brings us into covenant with God. Our offerings ratify that relationship with God each time we offer them to Him.

Foundation is everything to any structure. The structure of wealth creation requires the fundamentals listed in this section in order to recognize God as the source of our wealth.

Principles are like the glue that practically pull together the frame work of the structure and makes the structure physically stable and lasting.

SECTION THREE

Discover the practical application of wealth creation through your generosity.

CHAPTER EIGHT

PERPETUATING WEALTH FOR KINGDOM PURPOSES

Nature is Controlled By Laws

In Genesis 1 and 2, the account of creation shows that God in the beginning set in motion the Laws of multiplication and increase. Every creature including man was created with the potentials to reproduce itself. For six days God created everything on earth including man, and rested on the seventh day. The scripture says God ceased from all His works and rested on the seventh day. Does that mean that God is no longer in the business of creating new things? No. It means that He set in motion the laws that will acti- vate the latent potentials in each creature to multiply or reproduce its like. We are witnesses to some of God's creative miracles that cause us to exclaim that God is still in the business of creation! Adam was to multiply and fill the earth. (Genesis 1:28.)

God never intended to place a limitation on the abilities to increase in any of His creations. When He created sand He made it in abundance, the stars were created in abundance, the vegetation was created in abundance. And all creation has since multiplied itself. God is the God of continuity.

God's Blessings Should Not Begin and End With You

God promised Abraham that through him the families of the earth would be blessed. In Genesis 12:1-3: *"Now the Lord had said to Abram: Get out of your country, from your family and from your father's house, To a land that I will show you. I will make you a great nation; I will bless you And make your name great; And you shall be a blessing. I will bless those who bless you, And I will curse him who curses you; And in you all the families of the earth shall be blessed."*

God's promise to Abraham in Genesis 12 is that of giving him a nation and He continued to emphasize to him the fact that His blessings will be on his 'descendants'. In Genesis 15, when God spoke to him in a night vision, Abraham was reminding God of His promise to give him a 'son'. And God pointed Abraham to the sand on the seashore and the stars as the number of his children. But Abraham seemed to be hearing only the word, 'Son'. In blessing Abraham, God promised to multiply him and make him a blessing. God gave him Isaac and through Isaac came the nation of Israel. In spite of anti – Semitism in the world the people of Israel has been a great blessing in various fields of life.

We also like Abraham, often see God's promises to us as beginning and ending with us, while God wants us to see beyond ourselves to generations of our children yet unborn. Likewise, He wants us to share His blessings beyond our families to our communities, cities and nations. God is the God of abundance and continuity. The purpose of His blessings on our lives is to extend it to others. The blessings of God may begin with you but they do not end with you. It is His intent that you perpetuate His blessings in your life through your generosity. God is a generational God. We are His hands and feet on earth. The Lord has left the work of soul winning in our hands not in the hands of angels. We must learn to develop a large heart like our Father God to accommodate as many as possible.

> *"I will make you exceedingly fruitful; and I will make nations of you, and kings shall come from you. And I will establish My covenant between Me and you and*

> *your descendants after you in their generations, for*
> *an everlasting covenant, to be God to you and your*
> *descendants after you. Also I give to you and your*
> *descendants after you the land in which you are a*
> *stranger, all the land of Canaan, as an everlasting*
> *possession; and I will be their God."* Genesis 17:6-8

Noah left the Ark with eight members of his family that survived the flood and began to multiply till he filled the whole earth.

The Lord Jesus Christ did not die on the Cross-for the nation of Israel alone; He died for the whole world. He expects His harvest from all over the world. Our thinking must be global when we are ministering to others.

In the course of my studies, I discovered that the wealthy people of the world challenge each other to generosity. They champion philanthropic causes. When some of them do not know what to do with the extra money they accumulate, they sponsor many ungodly projects. Children of God should aspire to accumulate wealth for the kingdom and make the spreading of the gospel easy. It is obvious from our studies that God wants His Church to take the lead in causes of this nature. He does not want us as His children to limit His ability in us to multiply and increase us. You must learn to think like your Father God.

One of the covenant promises God gave to Abraham in the above passage of the Bible is that he will be a blessing and that through him nations will be blessed. This is the divine purpose for increase, that God's blessings on our lives will be perpetuated through our generosity. Abraham passed down his wealth to Isaac, Isaac to Jacob, Jacob to his sons, his sons to the nation of Israel and Israel to the rest of the world through the gift of Jesus Christ as the Savior of the world.

Your desire to create wealth must exceed selfish motives. Think of mission fields where the gospel is yet to be preached. You can sponsor the media ministry of your Pastor to enable her/him reach more souls beyond your local Church. In some cities of Nigeria in Africa, some individuals constructed church buildings single-handedly and handed over the keys to the buildings to their pastors. In our ministry, we were blessed with a couple who invested more than half the cost of construction of our large and beautiful church building. The blessing about this couple is that they refused to be celebrated openly, and they have remained loyal to my vision and me.

Wealth creation must be purpose driven. There should be a focus for accumulating wealth. For the child of God wealth should be for the furtherance of God's kingdom on earth.

I am personally pained by how some upcoming ministers in the Church Body in some parts of Africa are so dependent on the Christians in the West for most of their resources. We all have the potentials to multiply our gifts and talents. Friend, you must look inward for what you are seeking in others. There is in you an ability and divine enablement to be creative and to increase. What are needed are teachings of this nature that motivate the Christians to create wealth and give to God in covenant relationship.

Global events are showing us that doors to many nations are closing down on the gospel and effective evangelism is becoming more difficult. In such nations the believers are very few in number and are under severe persecution. They are unable to evangelize effectively. But with Information Technology, which has turned the world into a global village, communication travels now at the speed of light. So we must take advantage of the present day technology to reach the darkest and farthest parts of the world with the gospel. The costs of preaching the gospel through the airwaves is enormous, yet that is the fastest and safest way to reach those behind the iron curtains of false religions. So make more money for the kingdom!

Extras For The Society

> *"When the righteous prosper, the city rejoices; when the wicked perish, there are shouts of joy. Through the blessing of the upright a city is exalted, but by the mouth of the wicked it is destroyed"* Proverbs 11:10, 11

Wealth is all about extras!

It must be emphasized that wealth takes time to accumulate. It takes hard work with intelligence that comes with setting of attainable goals. Though Christians walk by faith they must seek knowledge concerning wealth creation. There are faith teachings that make wealth creation look like a lazy person's way of getting rich. There should be substance and information in our teachings in Church about wealth. Many who listen to these teachings do not have any other way to learn the truth about wealth except in church. Both the preacher and his listeners need information on regular basis.

Moreover before one can truly create wealth, he must be able to provide for his own basic needs of life because wealth is actually about extras. I must strike a balance here, I am not trying to say that you must be comfortable financially before you can engage in some financial exploits for the Lord. You can support the Lord's work at any level of your financial prosperity but to take cities and nations for the Lord will require wealth creation.

What a joy it will be when the church begins to see itself as a social catalyst especially in Africa and other Third World Countries. This will open the door to other realms of ministry. Jesus says the church is the light and the salt of the world. One is to illuminate the darkness of the society and the other to add flavor to the society. How appropriate it will be for the Church to provide Christian schools including universities, hospitals, and rehabilitation centers for society's dropouts and more. I know some Christians who not only sponsor mission projects in their ministries, they adopt mission fields and take care of specific projects on the fields. Jesus did not only minister spiritual things to people, He ministered material blessings to them also. The church should be involved in social activities that benefit their communities. Such exercises help promote the preaching of the gospel. When the righteous command wealth there is joy in the city because the wealth is invested into positive and purposeful projects that solve problems for the society.

We are engaged in providing primary schools in our rural mission fields where the communities are hostile to the gospel. The Schools gave us an inroad to their hearts, though the School fee for each child for three months is less than $10. The School building is all thatch and falls apart during the rains. A little extra will give such village a concrete School building and the Schoolteachers can each be paid as little as $150 a month, which will be a great blessing to them.

The principle of providing for the poor instituted by God Himself is for the preservation of the society. When the poor are being provided for, God is being honored. In Deuteronomy 15:11, the Bible says, *"For the poor will never cease from the land; therefore I command you, saying, 'You shall open your hand wide to your brother, to your poor and your needy, in your land.'"*

Taking Cities and nations for the Lord

"Therefore He said: "A certain nobleman went into a far country to receive for himself a kingdom and to return. So he called ten of his servants, delivered to them ten minas, and said to them, 'Do business till I come.' But his citizens hated him, and sent a delegation after him, saying, 'We will not have this man to reign over us.' And so it was that when he returned, having received the kingdom, he then commanded these servants, to whom he had given the money, to be called to him, that he might know how much every man had gained by trading. Then came the first, saying, 'Master, your mina has earned ten minas.' And he said to him, 'Well done, good servant; because you were faithful in a very little, have authority over ten cities.' And the second came, saying, 'Master, your minas has earned five minas.' Likewise he said to him, 'You also be over five cities.' Then another came, saying, 'Master, here is your mina, which I have kept put away in a handkerchief. For I feared you, because you are an austere man. You collect what you did not deposit, and reap what you did not sow.' And he said to him, 'Out of your own mouth I will judge you, you wicked servant. You knew that I was an austere man, collecting what I did not

deposit and reaping what I did not sow. Why then did you not put my money in the bank, that at my coming I might have collected it with interest?' And he said to those who stood by, 'Take the mina from him, and give it to him who has ten minas.' (But they said to him, 'Master, he has ten minas.) For I say to you, that to everyone who has will be given; and from him who does not have, even what he has will be taken away from him. But bring those enemies of mine, who did not want me to reign over them, and slay them before me." Luke 19:12-27

This parable of Jesus has to do with trading in money and His emphasis here is on investments as well as faithfulness on the part of the servants. There is a law I see in this parable: the ability to manage money determines your reward in life. Jesus did not in any way spiritualize the reward as some may want to do.

Intercessors have a better understanding of taking communities, cities, territories and nations for the Lord in prayers. When they take up a burden for a place, they sometimes would travel down to the specific place for a prayer walk and prophetic acts. Likewise, the Christian businessperson should take up the sponsorship of a city project or national project for the Lord, according to his/her ability. You may not necessarily go in person to such places if you are not called to go; but partner with the minister that God has called to go. It could be the sponsorship of a crusade or the construction of ministry facilities. The Lord Jesus gave the above parable speaking of rewarding His servants with the ruling of cities. I am so excited about the reward here – ruling over cities!

Can the Lord depend on you to adopt a community whose doors are shut to the gospel or even a city? Can He depend on you to take a nation for Him through your sponsorship of gospel projects? In this parable the rewards are on cities conquered.

CHAPTER NINE

SECURING YOUR FUTURE WITH A MONEY OR MATERIAL SEED

David Stopped the Spirit of Death With an Offering

"Therefore, the angel of the LORD commanded Gad to say to David that David should go and erect an altar to the LORD on the threshing floor of Ornan the Jebusite. So David went up at the word of Gad, which he had spoken in the name of the LORD. Now Ornan turned and saw the angel; and his four sons who were with him hid themselves, but Ornan continued threshing wheat. So David came to Ornan, and Ornan looked and saw David. And he went out from the threshing floor, and bowed before David with his face to the ground. Then David said to Ornan, "Grant me the place of this threshing floor, that I may build an altar on it to the LORD. You shall grant it to me at the full price, that the plague may be withdrawn from the people." But Ornan said to David, "Take it to yourself, and let my lord the King, do what is good in his eyes. Look, I also give you the oxen for burnt offerings, the

threshing implements for wood, and the wheat for the grain offering; I give it all." Then King David said to Ornan, "No, but I will surely buy it for the full price, for I will not take what is yours for the LORD, nor offer burnt offerings with that which costs me nothing." So David gave Ornan six hundred shekels of gold by weight for the place. And David built there an altar to the LORD, and offered burnt offerings and peace offerings, and called on the LORD; and He answered him from heaven by fire on the altar of burnt offering. So the LORD commanded the angel, and he returned his sword to his sheath." 1 Chronicles 21:18-27

The occasion of this passage was when David offended the Lord by taking a census of the people of Israel, which God forbade. This sin of the king cost Israel the lives of 70,000 people in three days. The Lord sent Prophet Gad to confront King David over the issue and placed three options of judgement before him.

David quickly owned up to his sin and repented, choosing to fall into the hands of God for judgement than to fall into the hands of men. So God sent three days of plague that claimed the lives of 70,000 people. On the third day of God's judgement, David caught up with the Angel of God in Ornan's field. As a covenant man with God, David knew to offer a sacrifice to the Lord to halt the spirit of death. What a lesson! He chose to make his offering a memorial and was determined to feel the pain of the cost (not a cheap offering). I had once given an offering of $1,000 to another ministry in response to a call to give, and instantly lost my joy. I could not sleep that night as the devil pounded my mind to confusion. My harvest came in the form of some godly, rewarding relationships that have been of immense blessing to me and have given me many open doors in the ministry. King David secured the healing of the nation and preservation of lives with these offerings to the Lord. The nation of Israel is good at preserving history; God taught them that from the beginning. The Church and indeed the individual believer in Christ should celebrate the divine interventions in their lives. Learn to make a memorial of the Lord's goodness and mercies. This is not about your temperament it is about honoring the Lord before the next generation.

Jacob Secured His Future with A Offering

> *"Then Jacob made a vow, saying, "If God will be with me, and keep me in this way that I am going, and give me bread to eat and clothing to put on, so that I come back to my father's house in peace, then the LORD shall be my God. And this stone which I have set as a pillar shall be God's house, and of all that You give me I will surely give a tenth to You."* Genesis 28: 20-22

Jacob sinned against his brother Esau by deceiving their blind, aged father and stealing away the blessing of Esau. This led to his sudden departure from home. As he was running for dear life, he had an encounter with the Lord Himself on his first night away from home. With the uncommon angelic visitation and hearing the voice of the Lord, he made the above vow to the Lord. He secured his future with the Lord with a vow of paying his tithe to the Lord.

The Passover Sacrifice Delivers A Nation From 430 Years of Bondage

> *"Your lamb shall be without blemish, a male of the first year. You may take it from the sheep or from the goats. Now you shall keep it until the fourteenth day of the same month. Then the whole assembly of the congregation of Israel shall kill it at twilight. And they shall take some of the blood and put it on the two doorposts and on the lintel of the houses where they eat it. Then they shall eat the flesh on that night; roasted in fire, with unleavened bread and with bitter herbs they shall eat it. Do not eat it raw, nor boiled at all with water, but roasted in fire – its head with its*

legs and its entrails. You shall let none of it remain until morning, and what remains of it until morning you shall burn with fire. And thus you shall eat it: with a belt on your waist, your sandals on your feet, and your staff in your hand. So you shall eat it in haste. It is the LORD's Passover. "For I will pass through the land of Egypt on that night and I will strike all the firstborn in the land of Egypt, both men and beast; and against all the gods of Egypt I will execute judgement; I am the LORD. Now the blood shall be a sign for you on the houses where you are. And when I see the blood, I will pass over you; and the plague shall not be on you to destroy you when I strike the land of Egypt." Exodus 12:5-13

"Now the sojourn of the children of Israel who lived in Egypt was four hundred and thirty years. And it came to pass at the end of the four hundred and thirty years – on that very same day – it came to pass that all the armies of the Lord went out from the land of Egypt. It is a night of solemn observance to the LORD for bringing them out of the land of Egypt. This is that night of the LORD, a solemn observance for all the children of Israel throughout their generations." Exodus 12: 40-42

Israel had been in bondage for 430 years in the land of Egypt. What bondage! What a stronghold this must have been on them. When God was set to deliver them it took ten powerful signs from God to shake up the whole land of Egypt. This was a battle between the gods of Egypt and God Himself in Exodus chapter 12. But it was not until the people of Israel cut a covenant with God Almighty that Egypt and its gods released Israel and let them go. Your sacrifices in the form of your offerings speak for you before the Lord and before the kingdom of darkness. There are times when it will take a quality and sizable offering from you to God to reverse the leanness of your purse and move you to the next level of financial breakthrough.

How do you come before the Lord at the Holy Communion table? It is a time to both renew and cut a fresh covenant with Him. While Israel cut this first Passover Covenant with the Lord God their request was deliverance from the powers holding them down in Egypt. The gods of Egypt held them down from pressing forward to God's Plans for them. They heard of their next level of progress from Moses, they could almost touch it yet it looked so impossible even after the ten signs and wonders performed through Moses. But that Passover Covenant with God broke the hold of the enemy off their backs.

Jesus the Passover Lamb of God had been slain from the foundations of the world opening up our way to God in Covenant relationship. At the Holy Communion table remember the blood of Jesus our Lord speaks and silences the voice of the enemy over your realm. Did the Lord deliver Israel from those powers in Egypt? Yes! He powerfully did. In the camp of their enemies it resulted in the death of the firstborn of Egypt. What a powerful way to let the Lord fight your battles for you. The next time you partake of the Holy Communion, take an offering as well as your needs to the Lord, especially the stubborn and lingering ones. I have done this several times when my household and I were under attacks from the spirit of death and the Lord graciously delivered us.

The Size of an Offering Secures a Throne

> *Now the king went to Gibeon to sacrifice there, for that was the great high place; Solomon offered a thousand burnt offerings on that altar. At Gibeon the LORD appeared to Solomon in a dream by night; and God said, "Ask! What shall I give you?" And Solomon said: "You have shown great mercy to Your servant David my father, because he walked before You in truth, in righteousness, and in uprightness of heart with You; You have continued this great kindness for him, and You have given him a son to sit on his throne, as it is this day. Now, O LORD my God, You have made your servant king instead of my*

father David, but I am a little child; I do not know how to go out or come in. And your servant is in the midst of Your people whom You have chosen, a great people, too numerous to be numbered or counted. Therefore give Your servant, an understanding heart to judge Your people that I may discern between good and evil. For who is able to judge this great people of Yours?" The speech pleased the LORD, that Solomon had asked for this thing. Then God said to him: "Because you have asked this thing, and have not asked long life for yourself, nor have asked riches for yourself, nor have asked the life of your enemies, but have asked for yourself understanding to discern justice, behold, I have done according to your words; see, I have given you a wise and under- standing heart, so that there has not been anyone like you before you, nor shall any like you arise after you. And I have also given you what you have not asked: both riches and honor, so that there shall not be anyone like you among the kings all your days. So if you walk in My ways, to keep My statutes, and My commandments, as your father David walked, then I will lengthen your days." 1 Kings 3:4-14

It has never ceased to amaze me that God would respond to the abundance of King Solomon's offerings by leaving heaven to come to earth just to show how touched He was. The fact that God Himself would not physically eat the offerings makes it look very much like our offerings today. God received the offerings but the Priests ate the offerings. God then gave King Solomon a signed blank check. Wow! I believe the quantity, quality as well as the heart of the giver in this case accounted for God's uncommon response. God gave King Solomon more than he requested from Him. He received the wisdom to rule God's people as well as wisdom for creating wealth for his kingdom and the nation of Israel.

Christians that are ruled by religious spirits cannot put up with preachers mentioning specific amounts of money to be brought as offerings before God, but they forget that God stipulated the quality, size and kind of offerings to be brought to His temple. You need to change your attitude towards your offerings.

Some years ago, I was going through a period of financial leanness both in the ministry and in my personal life. The period of leanness had reached its 7th year in 2000 and I was crying out to the Lord for His intervention. He gave me a personal breakthrough through the sale of personal real estate, which put a tithe of $3,000 USD into my hands. This was the highest tithe I was sowing in my life at that point. Because I made tithing a habit in my life since my teenage years, it was with much joy that I sowed this tithe. This particular seed of my tithe brought me a bountiful harvest of ideas, insight and concepts (I learnt this from Dr. Oral Roberts) on how to move into a lifetime of wealth creation. The Lord through this particular tithe gave me a stable and healthier financial life.

I learnt from Dr. Mike Murdock that I do not have financial problems rather, I have *wisdom* problems. I have since then gained so much wisdom on wealth matters and I am still learning.

> " And it happened when He was in a certain city, that behold, a man who was full of leprosy saw Jesus; and he fell on his face and implored Him, saying, "LORD, if You are willing, You can make me clean." Then He put out His hand and touched him, saying, "I am willing; be cleansed." Immediately the leprosy left him. And he charged him to tell no one, "But go and show yourself to the priest, and make an offering for your cleansing, as a testimony to them, just as Moses commanded." Luke 5:12-14

After healing this leper, Jesus sent him to the temple to show himself to the Priest. He also ordered him to take an offering as a testimony about his healing. Many do not know that they ought to take a quality offering to the Lord as they testify of His goodness and mercies on their lives. Always create a memorial with your seeds before the Lord.

The Dangers of Not Being Rich Towards God

> *"And He said to them, "Take heed and beware of covetousness: for one's life does not consist in the abundance of the things he possesses: Then He spoke a parable to them, saying: "The ground of a certain rich man yielded plentifully. And he thought within himself, saying, 'What shall I do, since I have no room to store my crops?' So he said, 'I will do this: I will pull down my barns and build greater, and there I will store all my crops and my goods. And I will say to my soul, "Soul, you have many goods laid up for many years; take your ease; eat, drink, and be merry." But God said to him, 'Fool! This night your soul will be required of you; then whose will those things be which you have provided?' "So is he who lays up treasure for himself, and is not rich toward God."* Luke 12:15-21

The rich man in the above parable excluded God from his business plans. He was a god to himself. He saw his wealth as a personal achievement, something that should be enjoyed by him alone. This is the result of covetousness, which is the same as idolatry. He was a fool for failing to realize that his life belonged to God and that the soil and the seed came from God. The wisdom and ability with which he succeeded was given to him by God. The favor that attracted investors to him was God's. After seed sowing, God gives the increase. The emphasis in this parable is in verse 21: *"...not being rich towards God."*

> *"For her rich men are full of violence, Her inhabitants have spoken lies, And their tongue is deceitful in their mouth."* Micah 6:12

Riches in wrong hands turn the possessor into a violent person.

> *"Neither their silver nor their gold shall be able to deliver them in the day of the LORD's wrath;"* Zephaniah. 1:18a

Trust in riches cannot deliver anyone from the hands of the Lord on the day of His judgement.

> *"Command those who are rich in this present age not to be haughty, nor to trust in uncertain riches but in the living God, who gives us richly all things to enjoy. Let them do good, that they be rich in good works, ready to give, willing to share, Storing up for themselves a good foundation for the time to come, that they may lay hold on eternal life."* 1Timothy 6:17-19

Apostle Paul gives us the key to accumulating wealth: do good works, give them away and increase thereby. These store up good treasures for eternity.

In concluding this chapter I want to point out that to perpetuate your wealth in God's kingdom, you have to be a blessing to others. Create more wealth for kingdom projects and tie expected harvests to your seeds. You should see your offerings as seeds, and if they are seeds, then there should be a harvest. If the harvest must be continuous then the sowing must be continuous. Do not eat up your seeds with your harvest!

CHAPTER TEN

TRUE RICHES VS THE LOVE OF MONEY

"He also said to his disciples: "There was a certain rich man who had a steward, and an accusation was brought to him that this man was wasting his goods. So he called him and said to him, "What is this I hear about you? Give an account of your stewardship, for you can no longer be steward." Then the steward said within himself, 'What shall I do? For my master is taking the stewardship away from me. I cannot dig; I am ashamed to beg. I have resolved what to do, that when I am put out of the stewardship, they may receive me into their houses.' "So he called every one of his master's debtors to him, and said to the first, 'How much do you owe my master?' And he said, 'A hundred measures of oil.' So he said to him, 'Take your bill, and sit down quickly and write fifty.' Then he said to another, 'And how much do you own?' So he said, 'A hundred measures of wheat.' And he said to him, 'Take your bill, and write eighty.' So the master commended the unjust steward because he had dealt shrewdly. For the sons of this world are *more shrewd in their generation than the sons of light. "And I say to you, make friends for yourselves by unrighteous mammon, that when you fail, they may receive you into an everlasting home. He who is faithful in what is least is faithful also in much; and he who is unjust in what is least is unjust also in much. Therefore if you have not been faithful in the unrighteous mammon, who will commit to your trust the true riches? And if you have not been faithful in what is another man's, who will give you what is your own? No servant can serve two masters; for either he will hate the one and love the other, or else he will be loyal to the one and despise the other. You cannot serve God and mammon." Luke 16:1-13*

W e were able to establish from the scriptures quoted in Chapter 4 that God gives riches to His people. We were also able to determine that riches in this context are basically material things.

In the above parable the Lord Jesus points to the fact that there are true riches. The presence of true riches implies that there are false riches. The state of a person's heart determines the kind of wealth he accumulates. A proud heart will break every rule just to make itself rich. Let's look at false riches from the scriptural perspective.

Riches Acquired Through Oppression

"And there was a great outcry of the people and their wives against their Jewish brethren. For there were those who said, "We, our sons, and our daughters are many; therefore let us get grain, that we may eat and live." There were also some who said, "We have mortgaged our lands and vineyards and houses, that we might buy grain because of the famine." There were also those who said, "We have borrowed money for the king's tax on our lands and vineyards. Yet now our flesh is as the flesh of our brethren, our children as their children; and indeed

we are forcing our sons and our daughters to be slaves, some of our daughters have been brought into slavery. It is not in our power to redeem them, for other men have our lands and vineyards." And I became very angry when I heard their outcry and these words. After serious thought, I rebuked the nobles and rulers, and said to them, "Each of you is exacting usury from his brother." So I called a great assembly against them. Nehemiah 5:1-7

"Woe to him who builds his house by unrighteousness. And his chambers by injustice, who uses his neighbor's service without wages, and gives him nothing for his work. Who says, 'I will build myself a wide house with spacious chambers, and cut out windows for it, paneling it with cedar and painting it with vermilion...Yet your eyes and your heart are for nothing but your covetousness, for shedding innocent blood, and practicing oppression and violence" Jeremiah 22:13-14, 17

Acquiring riches through oppression is present in every culture but thrives more in environments plagued with poverty. The mighty in these areas think they hold the destiny of others in their power. But God is the Deliverer of the weak from the hands of the powerful. The truth remains that the ungodly pursue wealth with the purpose of oppressing the weak in the society. A child of God can never have such a mind-set.

"This is the portion of a wicked man with God, And the heritage of oppressors, received from the Almighty: If his children are multiplied, it is for the sword; And his offspring shall not be satisfied with bread.

Those who survive him shall not be buried in death, And their widows shall not weep, Though he heaps up silver like dust, And piles up clothing like clay- He may pile it up, but the just will wear it, And the innocent will divide the silver. He builds his house like a moth, Like a booth which a watchman makes. The rich man will lie down, But not be gathered up; He opens his eyes, And he is no more.

Terrors overtake him like a flood; A tempest steals him away in the night. The east wind carries him away, and he is gone; It sweeps him out of his place.

It hurls against him and does not spare; Men shall clap their hands at him, And shall hiss him out of his place." Job 27:13-23

The book of Job tells of the reward of the wicked who oppresses the poor. Sometimes God's justice appears delayed and the righteous is looked down upon but you can be sure that God will vindicate His own. Proverbs 21:18 tells us, *"Sometimes the wicked are punished to save the godly, and the treacherous for the upright."* (New Living Translation).

"Getting treasures by a lying tongue is the fleeting fantasy of those who seek death." Proverbs. 21:6

Many are caught in this web of telling lies in their business in order to make more profit. Make it a principle *never* to tell lies. You can be wise in your dealings with people without lying.

The "Get Rich Quick" Syndrome

"One who increases his possessions by usury and extortion gathers it for him who will pity the poor"... *"A faithful man will abound with blessings, But he who hastens to be rich will not go unpunished"*... *"A man with an evil eye hastens after riches, And does not consider that poverty will come upon him."* Proverbs. 28:8,20,22

Here lies one of the greatest deceptions of acquiring wealth. A "get rich quick" scheme is the easiest way to destroy one's reputation and life. Wealth is acquired over a period of time. It requires adequate planning, the study of the principles of wealth creation, being a student of the rich and wealthy, (through personal contact or their products i.e. books, etc). Wealth acquired overnight grows wings and flies away, just like it came.

> *"Do not overwork to be rich; because of your own understanding, cease! Will you set your eyes on that which is not? For riches certainly make themselves wings; they fly away like an eagle toward heaven."* Proverbs 27:23,24

> *"Be diligent to know the state of your flocks, and attend to your herds; for riches are not forever, nor does a crown endue to all generations."* Proverbs 23:4,5

The statement *'Be diligent to know the state of your flocks, and attend to your herds'* means to pay attention to your business.

The Love of Money

> *"If anyone teaches otherwise and does not consent to wholesome words, even the words of our Lord Jesus Christ, and the doctrine which accords with holiness, he is proud, knowing nothing, but is obsessed with disputes and arguments over words, from which come envy, strife, reviling, evil suspicions, useless wranglings of men of corrupt minds and destitute of the truth, who suppose that godliness is a means of gain. From such withdraw yourself. Now godliness with contentment is great gain, For we brought nothing into this world, and it is certain we can carry nothing out. And having food and clothing, with these we shall be content. But*

those who desire to be rich fall into temptation and a snare, and into many foolish and harmful lusts which drown men in destruction and perdition. For the love of money is a root of all kinds of evil, for which some have strayed from the faith in their greediness, and pierced themselves through with many sorrows. But you, O man of God, flee these things and pursue righteousness, godliness, faith, love, patience, gentleness. Fight the good fight of faith, lay hold on eternal life, to which you were also called and have confessed the good confession in the presence of many witnesses... Command those who are rich in this present age not to be haughty, nor to trust in uncertain riches but in the living God, who gives us richly all things to enjoy. Let them do good, that they be rich in good works, ready to give, willing to share, storing up for themselves a good foundation for the time to come, that they may lay hold on eternal life." 1Timothy 6:3-13, 17-19

The above passage of the Bible has a two-edged effect. Firstly it speaks to people who pursue wealth and riches for the wrong reasons; they fall into many temptations. It is not the wealth or the riches that are wrong but the motives of the one in pursuit of them. Motives are everything in this particular passage of the Bible. Many have used this same passage to place limitations on believers in Christ in the area of wealth creation. Secondly in verses 17 – 19, Paul admonishes those who are rich on how to manage their riches; this obviously shows that he is not against the rich and wealthy.

The love of money makes money a god in people's lives. Many have literally killed others just to make more money. In Africa, there are true stories of people killing members of their own families in very fetish ways in order to make more money. The love of money is one of the major sources of crises in the home and in many organizations.

Some Christians have lost their faith in God while in pursuit of money. Their cases cannot annul or negate all we have studied in this book. Godliness with contentment is a great key to accumulation of wealth God's way.

The Rich Young Ruler

> *"Now as He was going out on the road, one came running, knelt before Him, and asked Him, 'Good Teacher, what shall I do that I may inherit eternal life?'*
>
> *So Jesus said to him, "Why do you call Me good? No one is good but One, that is, God. You know the commandments: 'Do not commit adultery,' 'Do not murder,' 'Do not steal.' 'Do not bear false witness,' 'Do not defraud,' 'Honor your father and your mother." And he answered and said to Him, "Teacher, all these things I have kept from my youth." Then Jesus, looking at him, loved him, and said to him, 'One thing you lack: Go your way, sell whatever you have and give to the poor, and you will have treasure in heaven; and come, take up the cross and follow Me." But he was sad at this word, and went away sorrowful, **for he had great possessions**. Then Jesus looked around and said to His disciples, "How hard it is for those who have riches to enter the kingdom of God!" And the disciples were astonished at His words. But Jesus answered again and said to them, "children, **how hard it is for those who trust in riches to enter the kingdom of God!** It is easier for a camel to go through the eye of a needle than for a rich man to enter the kingdom of God." And they were greatly astonished, saying among themselves, "Who then can be saved?"* Mark 10:17-31

The problem with this young ruler was that **his possessions possessed him!** Jesus was not in any way teaching against possessions, rather He pointed out here that this young ruler could not follow Him because of his **trust in riches.** This is the reason I have taken time in this study to point out God's intent for riches from the scriptures.

Deuteronomy 8:18 makes it absolutely clear that wealth creation for a child of God is a covenant with God: *"And you shall remember the LORD your God, for it is He who gives you power to get wealth, that He may establish His covenant which He swore to your fathers, as it is this day."* God enables you to create wealth for His Kingdom. The money and material resources needed for His Kingdom business are here on earth, not in heaven. Christians must put their trust in God as they create wealth for the Kingdom through God's ability in them.

This was one Bible passage that a lot of preachers used in the 1960s to dissuade their congregations from desiring to have wealth of any sort. Though I heard those teachings over and over again, I chose to study the Bible myself, and that set me free. Remember, *your motive is everything in wealth creation.* Proverbs 23:7 says, *"For as he thinks in his heart, so is he."*

> *"Those who love pleasure become poor; wine and luxury are not the way to riches."* Proverbs 21:17

This verse shows us another wrong motive for wealth creation: the love of pleasure. Loving pleasure leads to poverty and drunkenness. Every wrong reason for the acquisition of wealth is seen as the love of money. The *love* of money disqualifies anyone from wealth creation.

TRUE RICHES

Luke 16:11 says, *"Therefore if you have not been faithful in the unrighteous mammon, who will commit to your trust the true riches?"* Jesus raises this question, which implies that there is what God considers to be **true riches.** We shall again examine some passages of the scriptures on this topic.

Spiritual Blessings as Riches

> *"Therefore remember that you, once Gentiles in the flesh – who are called Uncircumcision by what is called the Circumcision made in the flesh by hands – that at that time you were without Christ, being aliens from the commonwealth of Israel and strangers from the covenants of promise, having no hope and without God in the world. But now in Christ Jesus you who once were far off have been brought near by the blood of Christ. For He Himself is our peace, who has made both one, and has broken down the middle wall of separation, having abolished in His flesh the enmity, that is, the law of commandments contained in the ordinances, so as to create in Himself one new man from the two, thus making peace, and that He might reconcile them both to God in one body through the cross, thereby putting to death the enmity. And He came and preached peace to you who were afar off and to those who were near. For through Him we both have access by one Spirit to the Father."* Ephesians 2:11-18

Your spiritual blessing begins when you make a quality decision to give your life to the Lord Jesus Christ, acknowledging His death on the cross as the price for your sin and the only way back to God. The price for your sin has already been paid by Jesus when He hung on that Cross for you, all you need do is confess your sins and ask for forgiveness of your past with a penitent heart and godly sorrow and invite Him right now into you heart. Ask Him to become the LORD over your life and promise to live for Him for the rest of your days on earth. I will suggest you find a quiet place to offer this prayer to the Lord. If you do so with all your heart, it marks the beginning of your spiritual blessings in God.

The above passage of the Bible points out that without Christ we are total strangers to God and we miss out of the <u>covenants of promise</u>. The death of Christ has brought us near to God and given us peace with God. I took this very step February 19, 1967; and the Lord has remained faithful to me. See the last page of this book for the steps to inviting Jesus Christ into your life.

> *"Blessed is the man who fears the Lord, who delights greatly in His commandments. His descendants will be mighty on earth; the generation of the upright will be blessed. Wealth and riches will be in his house, and his righteousness endues forever. Unto the upright there arises light in the darkness; he is gracious, and full of compassion, and righteous. A good man deals graciously and lends; he will guide his affairs with discretion. Surely he will never be shaken; the righteous will be in everlasting remembrance. He will not be afraid of evil tidings; his heart is steadfast, trusting in the LORD. His heart is established; he will not be afraid, until he sees his desire upon his enemies. He has dispersed abroad, he has given to the poor; his righteousness endues forever; his horn will be exalted with honor."* Psalm 112:1-9

This is a beautiful picture of a wealthy person, one who knows God with his household. Wealth starts with knowing God personally and being content with who you are in Christ. It begins within you before it is seen around you. If material things give fulfillment in life then the rich would never commit suicide. Inviting Christ into your life as your personal Lord and Savior marks the beginning of satisfaction and contentment in life as discussed above.

> *"There is one who makes himself rich, yet has nothing; and one who makes himself poor, yet has great riches. The ransom of a man's life is his riches, but the poor does not hear rebuke."* Proverbs 13:7-8

I believe this speaks of life in God that brings security and satisfaction in life.

"The crown of the wise is their riches, but the fool-ishness of fools is folly." Proverbs 14:24

"In the house of the righteous there is much treasure, but the revenue of the wicked is trouble. Better is little with the fear of God, than great treasure with trouble. Better is a dinner of herbs where love is, than a fatted calf with hatred." Proverbs 15:6, 16, 17

All the above scriptures from the book of Proverbs teach on the quality of life in God. They stress the fact that a man's life does not consist in the abundance of what he possesses materially or not. The knowledge of the Almighty is the greatest treasure on earth. Seek him first and His kingdom and you have wisdom to rule the material things of this life.

Ministry Gifts as True Riches

"Blessed be the God and Father of our Lord Jesus Christ, who has blessed us with every spiritual bless-ing in the heavenly places in Christ..." Ephesians 1:3

"Therefore if you have not been faithful in the unrighteous mammon, who will commit to your trust the true riches?" Luke 16:11

Talking about spiritual blessings, the callings and gifting of the Lord makes us rich in the sense that through us, many are not only led to the Lord but are also helped. The ability to manage our finan-cial success shows that God has qualified us for greater gifts in His kingdom. The gifts of the Holy Spirit in 1 Corinthians 12 are trea-sures to be managed for the Lord. The fivefold ministry gifts of Ephesians 4:11 are offices to be managed for the Lord with great caution. Have you seen a minister of the gospel managing a large and multifaceted ministry, know that she or he is good and account-able in money matters?

The spiritual gifts are what I believe the Lord Jesus referred to as *true riches* in the parable of the unjust steward, because of their eternal values.

Friends as Wealth and Riches

It is said that if you have just one friend in life, you are rich. There are friends and then there are *friends*. I consider a friend as one who sticks closer than a biological brother. When you find one, place a high premium on that relationship. Protect and celebrate it. It takes years to build or cultivate a healthy relationship with anyone. And true Friendship is a gift.

> *"Wealth makes many friends, but the poor is separated from his friend."* Proverbs 19:4

This verse sounds like the words of Jesus in the parable of the unjust steward: *"And I say to you, make friends for yourselves by unrighteous mammon, that when you fail, they may receive you into an everlasting home."* (Luke 16:9). There is wisdom in using what I call the 'money power' to build healthy and lasting relationships that are capable of sustaining one in rainy days.

> *"A friend loves at all times, and a brother is born for adversity."* Proverbs 17:17

> *"A man who has friends must himself be friendly, but there is a friend who sticks closer than a brother."* Proverbs 18:24

> *"Faithful are the wounds of a friend, but the kisses of an enemy are deceitful. Ointment and perfume delight the heart, and the sweetness of a man's friend gives delight by hearty counsel. Do not forsake your own friend or your father's friend, nor go to your brother's house in the day of your calamity; better is a neighbor nearby than a brother far away. As iron sharpens iron, so a man*

sharpens the countenance of his friend." Proverbs
27:6, 9-10, 17

*"Two are better than one, because they have a good
reward for their labor. For if they fall, one will lift
up his companion. But woe to him who is alone
when he falls, for he has no one to help him up.
Again, if two lie together, they will keep warm; but
how can one be warm alone? Though one may be
overpowered by another, two can withstand him.
And a threefold cord is not quickly broken."*
Ecclesiastes 4:9-12

These scriptures show us the values of a friend. Cultivate
healthy relationships. Friends may be younger than you are; some
may be in your age group, yet others may be older than you are.
You can learn from any of them.

The Gift of Parents as Wealth

*"Honor your father and your mother, that your days
may be long upon the land which the LORD your
God is giving you."* Exodus 20:12

Honor for father and mother is a fundamental factor in creating
wealth on earth. This is the first commandment of God with
promise. This is one relationship you must protect and honor. You
must find a way to honor your parents while they are alive. Some
people do not have the luxury of having one or both parents alive;
however honor whoever stands in for you as parents. Wealthy
parents leave their wealth to their children who had honored them.
Making your parents your enemies will backfire. I am aware that
there are parents who are more of heartaches to their children and
are very ungrateful, yet God's promise in that commandment does
not have a condition attached to it. Ask the Lord for wisdom on
how best to honor them, even if in spite of them.

The Gift of Children as Wealth

> *Lo, children are an heritage from the LORD; and the*
> *fruit of the womb is his reward. As arrows are in the*
> *hand of a mighty man, so are children of one's youth.*
> *Happy is the man who hath his quiver full of them;*
> *they shall not be ashamed, but they shall speak with*
> *the enemies in the gate. Psalm 127:3-5 (KJV).*

Children's children are a crown to the aged, and parents are the pride of their children. Proverbs 17:6.

Children are treasures from the Lord and must be seen as such not as burdens because of our responsibilities towards them. Bless your children daily, speak into their lives. One of the wisest things to do on earth is to be a friend to all your children. Treasure your time with each one of them.

CHAPTER ELEVEN

THE INHERENT
POWER OF THE SEED

This chapter unlocks in a practical way all that we have studied so far. Having taken time to explain and expatiate on God's original intent for the creation of man, which is to *rule over the three spheres of this planet;* I shall now proceed to releasing the keys to unlocking your wealth. The laws of sowing and reaping are the underlying factors to releasing your wealth.

God Commands the Land to Always Release Your Harvest

> *"Then God blessed them, and God said to them, 'Be fruitful and multiply; fill the earth and subdue it; have dominion over the fish of the sea, over the birds of the air, and over every living thing that moves on the earth.' And God said, 'See, I have given you every herb that yields seed which is on the face of all the earth, every tree whose fruit yields seed; to you it shall be for food. Also, to every beast of the earth, to every bird of the air, and to everything that creeps on the earth, in which there is life, I have given every green herb for food'; and it was so."* Genesis 1:28-30

At creation God set laws in motion that control and regulate everything, such as the law of gravity, laws that regulate the seasons, the day and night, sowing and reaping, etc. These laws have never failed and never will. In the law of sowing and reaping, God has already given the *land* a command to produce whenever seed is *sown* into it. He has given man *seed* (verse 29) to sow, so it is now left for man to activate the *laws* that will release his harvest. In verse 29 God placed an emphasis on *"every herb that yields seed*... and ... *every tree whose fruit yields seed"* It is *seed* that God has given to man and that seed must be *sown* into the ground before a harvest can be expected.

God Is In the Business of Supplying and Multiplying Seed, Not Harvest.

> *"Now may He who supplies* **seed** *to the* **sower**, *and bread for food,* **supply** *and* **multiply** *the* **seed** *you have* **sown** *and increase the fruits of your righteousness."* 2 Corinthians 9:10

We see again from this verse that God supplies *seed* (not the harvest) to the *sower* (not to everybody). The *sower* is the one that receives the bread for food. God supplies and multiplies the *seed* (not the harvest) that you have *sown*.

As long as the seed remains in your hands there can be no harvest. Please understand that these laws have always been at work and you just need to activate them to have the desired results. If you decide to pursue your harvest through only fasting and praying while withholding your seeds, you will receive no harvest. God will always multiply the seed sown.

Four Types of soils

In the parable of the sower (Matthew 13:6-8), Jesus teaches about 4 types of soils: (a) wayside, (b) rocky places, (c) thorny places and (d) good soil. It is important you identify your soil before sowing. The more fertile the soil, the greater the harvest.

In the parable of the talents, the wicked servant's talent was taken from him and given to the wise investor who had more returns from his trading. Sow into a higher anointing... sow into a greater vision than yours... the returns will be worth it!

Your Type of Harvest is Determined by Your Type of Seed

(i) Seed types: corn, mango, orange, car, house, naira, dollar... seed will always produce its kind (Genesis 1:11).
(ii) Quality of seed: Leviticus 22:20: *"Whatsoever has a defect, you shall not offer, for it shall not be acceptable on your behalf."* Another factor that affects harvest is the quality of your seed sown. Decaying seeds will produce little or no harvest at all.
(iii) Quantity of seed: the size of your seed determines the size of your harvest (2 Corinthians 9:6)... sowing sparingly opposed to sowing bountifully. The law of measure comes to play here.

Pre-Plan Your Seed

1. Ask the Holy Spirit what to sow at any given time. Paul admonished the church in Corinth to pre-plan their offerings one year before the collection (2 Corinthians 9:1-5). We have learnt that our offerings are forms of ratifying our covenants with God, so it should not be done at the spur of the moment. Farmers plan their seeds - type, quality, quantity and type of soil – before sowing. You determine the type of house you want to build before the breaking of ground. Your architect produces the drawing and in some cases the model of the house before the cost can be determined.
2. Give your seed an assignment (DNA). The rich woman in Elisha's life gave her seed no DNA until the prophet insisted on her naming her harvest – a son (2 Kings 4:8-17). I had often wondered why Jesus would see a blind beggar crying out for help, and ask him what he wanted from Him. Jesus wanted the blind man to name his harvest. Blind Bartimaeus

could have chosen money as his harvest or simply mere recognition from Jesus, but he chose his sight. (Mark 10:46).

Harvest Comes in the Measure With Which You sow

The seed *must be sown* if there is to be a harvest. Seeds eaten or withheld can never yield any harvest.

> *"Give, and it shall be given unto you: good measure, pressed down, shaken together, and running over shall men give into your bosom. For with the same measure that ye mete withal it shall be measured to you again."* Luke 6:38 (King James Version)

The second part of this verse shows us how our harvest is measured. When we give it is given in the name of the Lord to *men*. God has no need of a car in heaven nor a house nor money, so we give to *men in God's name*. Man is made of the dust of the earth so he is the ground we sow into. And the harvest comes from *men* into your bosom. Please note that your harvest may not necessarily come from the recipient of your gift; it is God who will cause men to give into your bosom.

When King Solomon offered one thousand burnt offerings on one altar in a service (2 Chronicles 1:6), it was the priest that ate the sacrifices but Solomon received the divine visitation. Do not be overly concerned with who eats (or rather, spends) your sacrifice. Give your offerings out of your needs to the Lord. Solomon's need was wisdom to lead God's great people. King David offered his sacrifice at the field of Araunah out of the need to keep death away from the nation of Israel at that point in time (2 Samuel 24). Apostle Paul admonishes not to give out of necessity but rather to give cheerfully. (2 Corinthians 9:7).

In Luke 6:38, Jesus emphasizes the fact that the measure with which you measure your seeds will determine the measure of harvest returned to you. When you give offerings in tens of dollars or its equivalent, you receive the same measure in multiples. When you give in hundreds of dollars or its equivalent, you receive the same measure of multiples. When you give in thousands of dollars or its equivalent, you receive the same measure of multiples. The same goes for when you give in millions of dollars or its equivalent: you reap in the same measure. Notice that God does not *add, subtract* or *divide*. Rather, He *multiplies*. Give a healthy car away and you receive a healthy car or its equivalent in multiples. Once I learnt this principle of sowing and reaping, my regular offerings have risen gradually over the years, as have my tithes. I give in the measure of my expected harvest. *God multiplies your hundreds according to the hundreds you have sown and your thousands accordingly.* Give in the name of the Lord and the harvest is yours for the taking.

The measure with which you give is the measure with which you receive. Never ask God for things; never ask Him for a harvest. Rather, ask Him for the *seed!* The seed will produce the harvest. There is inherent power in every seed. Get to your next level in life with "the measure you give" What you need is hidden in the seed – car, house, marriage, children – always ask the Lord for *seed to sow.*

The joy of giving to the Lord is that His harvest is measureless: *"...exceedingly (immeasurably), abundantly above, all we ask or think, according to the power that works in us,"* (Ephesians 3:20).

One of our young ladies in church called me one morning in the course of writing this book. She had just received her law degree certificate from the Law School a few minutes prior to the call. She was beside herself with joy and gratitude to God. She kept exclaiming, "It was the seed!" She shared how tough it is to pass the examinations for the law degree and she was not confident while preparing for and writing the examinations. She fulfilled her part of the preparations, but said she kept cutting covenants with the Lord with her offerings. She knew she did not fare too well in some of her papers but she kept sowing covenant seeds with monies that came into her hands even as a student and sometimes she was left with no money at all. Her joy drew me to tears, seeing a young lady in her early twenties believing God for what older people would stage a debate. She kept shouting, "The seed works!"

Waiting For Your Harvest

The period between seed sowing and harvest is the most trying times for the Sower. The farmer does not go to sleep after sowing; the work continues even as he waits for his harvest. More money is spent to rid the tender growing blades of unwanted weeds. In some cases an eye must be kept on the birds of the air that will seek to destroy the harvest. Re-visit chapter 2 of this book. The birds of the air represent *communication* – the voice of fear and doubt. More money is spent planning on expansion as a result of the anticipated harvest, more laborers may be hired, and so on. We often misunderstand what this period stands for in the life of every sower.

How to wait for your harvest

- Wait in *faith*. Abraham's Covenant Offering to God (Gen. 15); while in the presence of God in this night vision, Abraham had to chase the birds of the air away from his sacrifice. God did nothing about the birds; Abraham had to do something about them. He sure waited in *faith* till he received the harvest of the prophesies of four generations of his descendants...assurance of a great future. When the Shunemite rich woman's harvest (her miracle son obtained through her Prophet's offering to Elisha) was stolen by death she received him back by *faith*. The widow who gave Elijah a prophet's offering in obedience to God's command at one point also lost the harvest of her son to death but she received him back to life by *faith*.
- Stand on the *Word of God*. Waiting for your harvest requires standing on the Word of God that cannot fail. Fill your mind with the Word of God – Bible on tape, confessions of faith, etc.
- Be persistent in *prayer*, knowing your hope in Him shall not make you ashamed (Romans 5:5). Be dogged in prayers. Hannah in the book of Samuel was persistent in prayers till she received a word from Eli. Bind Bartimaeus would not give up until Jesus called for him.
- *Keep sowing* to sustain the harvest.

● *Worship is a powerful tool at this season of waiting for your harvest.* Silence every other voice through worship, slot in that worship tape and lay face down before the Lord like Job and declare, "I am yours Lord."

> *"Then the Lord will be zealous for His land, and pity His people. The Lord will answer and say to His people, "Behold, I will send you grain and new wine and oil, and you will be satisfied by them; I will no longer make you a reproach among the nations. "But I will remove far from you the northern army, and will drive him away into a barren and desolate land, with his face towards the eastern sea and his back towards the western sea; his stench will come up, and his foul will rise, because he has done monstrous things." Fear not, O land; be glad and rejoice for the LORD had done marvelous things! Do not be afraid you beasts of the field; for the open pastures are springing up, and the tree bears its fruit; the fig tree and the vine yield their strength. Be glad then, you children of Zion, and rejoice in the LORD your God; for He has given you the former rain, and He will cause the rain to come down for you – the former rain, and the latter rain in the first month. The threshing floors shall be full of wheat, and the vats shall overflow with new wine and oil. "So I will restore to you the years that the swarming locust has eaten, the crawling locust, the consuming locust and the chewing locust, my great army which I sent among you. You shall eat in plenty and be satisfied, and praise the name of the LORD your God who has dealt wondrously with you; and My people shall never be put to shame. Then you shall know that I am in the midst of Israel: I am the LORD your God and there is no other. My people shall never be put to shame. "And it shall come to pass afterward that I will pour out my Spirit upon all*

flesh; your sons and your daughters shall prophesy,
your old men shall dream dreams, your young men
shall see visions." Joel 2:18-28

Three Specific Harvests

Joel prophesied three harvests in the above passage of the Bible: a financial harvest, a harvest of miracles and a harvest of souls. All three will manifest in these last days of the Church. The Church has emphasized the harvest of souls over the years and treats the harvest of miracles as just "signs of the End Times," nothing is ever mentioned about the financial harvest.

We have witnessed in our time some amazing harvests of souls through mass citywide crusades, and the mass media has become a mighty tool for evangelism. The harvest of miracles will bring in financial harvests, which in turn will bring in multiples of harvests of souls into God's kingdom. The Church must take advantage of the media ministry to push the gospel of our Lord Jesus Christ.

The Church is about to witness a phenomenal multiplication of the three harvests mentioned above. The coming of the Lord sure is closer than we can imagine, so we must go for the harvest!

Sowers are bound to receive seeds from God knowing that they will obediently sow into the good soil. God honors His faithful sowers with bountiful harvests. Why not change your stand today and try the Lord is this matter of creating wealth for His Kingdom.

SECTION THREE

God is the God of continuity. It is His intent that you perpetuate His blessings on your life through your generosity. The costs of preaching the gospel through the airwaves is enormous, yet that is the fastest and safest way to reach those behind the iron curtains of false religions of the world. So make more money for the kingdom!

To perpetuate your wealth in God's kingdom, you have to be a blessing to others. Create more wealth for kingdom projects and tie expected harvests to your seeds. You should see your offerings as seeds, and if they are seeds, then there should be a harvest. If the harvest must be continuous then the sowing must be continuous. Do not eat up your seeds with your harvest!

The money and material resources needed for God's Kingdom business are here on earth, not in heaven.

Wealth creation should be God – centered and not out of love for money.

Treasure and protect the True Riches in your life.

Continuity is so crucial to any endeavor in life and to sustain your wealth is to make the Kingdom of God the central focus of the excicerse.

CONCLUSION

I can imagine you heaving a sigh of relief, now totally free from the doctrines of men. I am sure you agree that the Bible is a gold mine often neglected by the very people it is meant to bless. Ignorance is the greatest disease in the Church today. I challenge you today to take God by His Word concerning your calling to create wealth for His kingdom.

Global events point to the imminent return of our Lord and Savior Jesus Christ, and more Bible prophecies are being fulfilled daily. Watching recent events, one can see the nation of Israel beginning to accept the Gentile Church. Of note is the recent celebration of the Feast of Shelters in the land of Israel (October 2004). Many Christians from the Western World gathered in Israel for that feast. From the media reports of Pat Robertson's 700 Club, both Christians and Jews celebrated together. God is beginning to remove the 'veil' from the eyes of Israel. This should put the Church on high alert. The coming of our Lord is drawing nearer than we may realize.

This calls for urgency in the way and manner we preach the gospel to the entire world. Are you called to finance the gospel of God's Kingdom? Increase your seed sowing. God so loves people and does not want any to perish. Every ethnic group, tongue and tribe must be given the opportunity to hear the gospel of Christ at least once in their lifetime. You do not really have to go in person but your products can penetrate lives, homes and communities in nations you may never have opportunity to visit.

Can God depend on you to take cities or nations by sponsoring Christian crusades for Him? Would you walk up to your minister today and make a commitment to partner with him or her in this Kingdom business? Let us storm the 'birds of the air' — the media —and lift Jesus up there that He might draw *all* people to Himself. Let the marketplace Christian storm the 'fish of the sea' for bigger catches – much funding is needed today to make Jesus known. Possessing the land signifies being established in order to mature the Church. Every ministry needs an operational base to enable it to 'occupy'. The teaching ministry of the Church is in dire need today in order to make disciples for the Lord.

Do not silence the voice of the Holy Spirit speaking to you today. There are people that may never enter their destiny until you arise and take your position of rulership in this Kingdom business. You cannot afford to meet the Master with excuses; you were *'created to rule'*.

A FINAL WORD
FROM THE AUTHOR

Friend,

What joy to have shared with you these great truths of the gospel of our Lord Jesus Christ! I know these teachings have changed your perspective on matters relating to funding God's Kingdom with your material resources. You can now comprehend your divine purpose as having been *'created to rule'* the three spheres of this life. I shall be glad to hear from you about how this book has helped you or someone you know.

Would you take up your pen now and write me today? Alternatively, you may send me an email message.

Your Friend,

Grace Oby Johnson

Friend,

I want to invite you to give your life to the Lord Jesus Christ. Take the following steps:

- Come to the Lord Jesus right now with a broken heart and ask Him for forgiveness of your sins. It does not matter how grievous your sins might be, He invites you in the book of Isaiah 1:18: *"Come now, and let us reason together," says the LORD, "Though your sins are like scarlet, they shall be as white as snow; though they are red like crimson, they shall be as wool..."* Confess your sins to the Lord and ask Him to cleanse you with His blood. Feel sorry for your life style as you cry to the Lord for a change.
- Invite the Lord Jesus into your life to be your Lord and Savior.
- Believe He has heard and answered your prayers, thank Him for that; Isaiah 44:22: *"I have blotted out, like a thick cloud, your transgressions. And like a cloud, your sins. Return to me, for I have redeemed you."*
- Start a daily reading of God's word (the Bible). Begin from the gospel of John.
- Write down lessons you learn from God's word.
- Find a Bible believing Church in your area and join in their fellowship
- Tell your friends of this experience of a new life in Christ Jesus.
- Write me and share your testimony.

LOGOS AFLAME MINISTRIES

8-10 LOGOS CHURCH STREET.
OSAPA. LEKKI
P.O.BOX 8245, IKEJA. LAGOS
NIGERIA.
Tel. 234-1-792-7829

Website:
http:// www.gracejohnsonministries.org

TEMPORARY ADDRESS
P.O. BOX 2435
SOUTH BEND, IN 46680
pastor_gracej@yahoo.com

PICTURES OF MY OTHER BOOKS

The Holy Spirit & You (French translation available)

Fighting the Battles of Life
Deliverance From the Spirit of Witchcraft

Printed in the United States
76045LV00006B/349-396